FROZEN STIFF

FROZEN STIFF

Follow your dreams....

Sherry ~~Sherry~~
Shahan ~~Shahan~~

DELACORTE PRESS

DELACORTE PRESS
Published by
Bantam Doubleday Dell Publishing Group, Inc.
1540 Broadway
New York, New York 10036

Library of Congress Cataloging-in-Publication Data

Shahan, Sherry.
Frozen stiff / by Sherry Shahan.
    p.   cm.
    Summary: Cousins Cody and Derek take a kayak trip in Alaska
and find themselves battling the raw elements of an untamed
wilderness.
    ISBN 0-385-32303-4
    [1. Alaska—Fiction. 2. Kayaking—Fiction. 3. Survival—
Fiction. 4. Cousins—Fiction.] I. Title.
PZ7.S52784Fr   1998
[Fic]—dc21   97-33048
                                                            CIP
                                                             AC

The text of this book is set in 11.5-point Berling.
Book design by Semadar Megged
Manufactured in the United States of America
September 1998
10 9 8 7 6 5 4 3 2 1
BVG

Especially for Christine Peterson,
intrepid and "enlightened" traveler

CANADA

Mt. Cook

Disenchantment
Bay

Mt. Hubbard

HUBBARD
GLACIER

SAINt ELIAS
MOUNTAINS

ALASKA

*helicopter

Gilbert
POINT

Kayak
capsize

YAKUTAT
BAY

Fishing
Shelter *

Cabin
*
2nd
Camp

icebergs

TONGASS
NATIONAL
FOREST

Yakutat

1st
Camp*

Russell
Fjord

"Shark"
encounter

Pickup
Truck

GULF OF ALASKA

MAP BY

DEREK

1

Cody tried opening the door of the old pickup so that it wouldn't squeak. Darn! She should have greased the rusty hinges. Everything about the old truck was rusted and worn out. No wonder, with a constant gray mist strangling the sunshine in Southeast Alaska.

"Pssst! Derek!" she whispered through the rolled-down window. "Come on!"

Her cousin slammed the cabin door as always. He was as quiet as a bear breaking into a grocery store. How could they sneak off in a stolen truck when he was so noisy? Well, Cody thought wistfully, it wasn't really stolen. Just on temporary loan, without permission.

Cody tossed the last duffel onto the flatbed already loaded with canvas bags holding a tent, two sleeping bags, and other camping gear. There was enough food to last a week, though they would only be gone two nights. Two nights was the amount of time both their mothers would be in Juneau picking up supplies for Yakutat Lodge and Tavern.

Two nights alone on the fjord, without any adults. They would paddle their kayaks down the steep-sided seawater passage until their muscles ached, then scout a sandy bank and pitch their tent—the image warmed Cody's insides. But first they had to drive to the fjord without getting caught.

"Quiet!" Cody hushed her cousin as the door on the passenger's side creaked open. "We have to leave before someone from the lodge sees us."

Cody's mother managed the tavern during the summer, so Cody spent all three months with her mother in a log cabin behind the lodge. The cabin was private, although people were always coming and going and rarely knocked.

Cody's space was a small loft upstairs, her sleeping bag spread on a foam pad. Her clothes were stacked in discarded cartons. Sometimes, since the divorce, that was how she felt. Discarded with a bold *D*.

Cody often wished she had a real bed and a dresser in Yakutat for her things, so that the loft upstairs would seem more permanent. But mostly she wished they lived in Alaska year-round. Then she wouldn't have to think about her life on the "outside," a term Alaskans used for any spot outside the state. Sunny California? She smiled at the irony. That was what other people called it. For three years now, any thought Cody had of the Golden State and its inhabitants—especially certain inhabitants—had been tarnished with bad memories.

Cody flicked on the windshield wipers. "I hate the way the truck rattles," she told Derek while he tried buckling the broken seat belt. "It sounds like it's saying *Help! I'm being stolen!*"

The truck splashed through the potholes that pit-
ted the narrow alley between the main lodge and the
smaller cabins out back. Cody watched the cabins fade
into the gray mist in her rearview mirror. For a moment she wondered if she'd ever see the buildings
again. Then she pushed the idea from her mind.

"Can I drive?" Derek asked, raking damp hair out
of his eyes. Burnt-toast-brown hair and dark eyes, just
like her older brother, Patterson. Being around Derek
kept her from missing Patterson so much. "When
we're out of town?" Derek was saying. "Okay?"

"When did you learn to drive?" Cody turned onto
the unmarked road that twisted through an old forest
that had recently been clearcut. There was nothing
now but acres of pitiful stumps. "You aren't even old
enough for a permit."

Normally Cody would have laughed at someone
calling Yakutat a town, with its tiny population of
750. There wasn't even a road to the rest of the state;
the only way in and out was by boat or plane. Still,
Yakutat was the only community within hundreds of
miles of the fjord. A one-hangar airport and its narrow
landing strip bordered the lodge parking lot. Add a
grocery store, Laundromat, and post office. That was
about it.

"*You* don't have a license," Derek pointed out.

"That's different," she said. "I've driven this truck
three summers now." In her mind she added the
words *ever since the divorce*.

Cody sometimes drove the truck to the beach
even though she didn't have a driver's license. It

wasn't any big deal. The native kids started driving when they could barely see over the dashboard.

When a van pulled out from a wooded area Cody slumped in the seat. Normally she would have waved and whistled. But not with two of the lodge's foldup kayaks in back, one of their bear horns, and a water purifer. All borrowed without permission.

The uneasy feeling in her gut told her she should have called her mother in Juneau. She should have asked to spend a couple of days camping in the fjord. Mrs. Lewis might have said okay—the laid-back Alaskan lifestyle had changed her in so many ways. Giving Cody more freedom was one of them. Still, it was Aunt Jessie's and Derek's first visit to the forty-ninth state, and they had only been in Yakutat ten days. Aunt Jessie would have said no loud enough to be heard back in California.

"Mom doesn't even like it when I leave the lodge," Derek had argued two days ago when the idea began unfolding. "She's all freaked out about grizzly bears. And close encounters of the moose kind."

"What would she say if she knew you hitch-hiked?" Cody had asked.

"That was only one time. Besides, it was an emergency."

"Surfing? Some emergency."

"Waves like that don't hit California every day," he'd said. "And I didn't have a ride to the beach."

"You've always been too trusting, Derek."

So the cousins had made a bet to settle the argument about asking permission. If Cody won, she'd ask her mom about the camping trip. If Derek won, they wouldn't ask. Cody lost. How had Derek known that a caribou was the same animal as a reindeer?

"Come on," Derek pleaded. "You can teach me to drive."

Cody sucked in a deep breath, trying to calm her nerves. She hated sneaking around. "Forget it."

Only one outfitter had a wilderness permit to lead expeditions into Russell Fjord Wilderness of the Tongass National Forest. Cody had gone with their expeditions many times, as an unofficial assistant. She had helped set up tents, cook meals, break camp. "Pack it in. Pack it out." She'd heard the rule a dozen times.

No trips were scheduled this late in the summer, she knew, so no one would see them once they were on the water. And they were planning to return home hours before the flight from Juneau landed late Sunday night with their mothers.

"Just a little way. Plee-eease?" Derek kept at her. "I won't go fast."

"You're such a nag," she said lightly. "Maybe on the way home if there's time."

The old truck pushed through the heavy mist to a sloppy dirt road, which twisted alongside a patch of berry vines until it dead-ended. Bears hadn't raided this patch yet: The vines were still bright with salmonberries. No one used this narrow road except the outfitters.

Cody eased the front of the truck into the tangled vines and hid the keys under the back bumper. "Let's start unloading," she said, looping the arms of her rain slicker around her waist. A pair of shorts with Velcro pockets covered her dance tights. If the sun came out, she would shed the tights. "We have a three-quarter-mile hike to the beach. It'll take a few trips to carry all the gear."

On the last trip to the beach Cody lost one of her knee-high rubber boots in a soupy muskeg, a swampy hole of dark decayed matter. Her boot was sucked right off her foot. "Darn. Now my only pair of socks is drenched." Wet socks produced instant blisters. "How many socks did you pack?" she hollered back to Derek, who was behind her.

Derek was wobbling in a mudhole studded with knotted roots. There wasn't much of a trail and his heavy pack made it difficult to balance. "None."

"You aren't wearing socks with your boots?" She couldn't believe it. "Don't you think your feet will get cold?"

Derek had figured out how to rest without taking off his pack, by leaning against a tree. "What for? We're going camping. Not to a Christmas parade."

Cody shook her head. "The kayaks will be on water with glacial runoff. *Glacial*, get it? As in a frozen river? Ever hear of frostbite?" No one got frostbite this late in summer unless there was a freak storm. Still, she thought it sounded impressive.

Derek tried to shrug but it was impossible with the heavy pack.

"Did you bring long underwear?" She hated sounding like Aunt Jessie but this was important.

Preparation wasn't everything in the wilderness. It was the *only* thing.

"My underwear is none of your business," he shot back.

Cody hadn't said anything about his jeans, which would be totally useless. Much too heavy. Once they got wet they never dried out. But no socks? Stupid! She was just as mad at herself for not packing an extra pair.

Something deep in her gut told her to turn back, to forget the whole thing. She'd been camping, with the outfitters, many times, and she'd go with them many more. A trip that started out badly would only get worse. She knew that for a fact.

Why not spend the next two days in the lodge, watching videos and munching microwave popcorn? If they got bored, they could count drunk fishermen on holiday from the Lower Forty-eight as they staggered out of the tavern.

Derek finally caught up. He helped pull her boot out of the boggy hole. It made a sound like a sink draining.

"Tell me again what a glacier looks like up close," he said.

"Not now." Cody hated being such a grouch but nothing made her as miserable as wet socks. "We're leaving this load here. Then we're going down to the beach to collect the rest of our gear. We're heading back to the lodge."

"What do you mean? This is the last of the stuff

and the truck is half a mile back. *Uphill.*" The sun went behind some heavy clouds, and the scream of mosquitoes rose from the trees. Derek swiped at the air several times. "If these suckers are going to follow us they could at least carry something."

Cody laughed at that one. "Some people think they should be named the state bird."

It was as if the mosquitoes had invited all their friends for the human feast. Cody batted wildly to keep them out of her eyes. "Get away!" she shouted. "Now I know what nose hairs are for . . . to filter out bugs."

Derek's forehead was already a mass of bites. "I think I swallowed one."

"The mosquito nets for our hats are in the duffel on the beach," she hollered, and stumbled downhill toward the strand of coarse sand. "And I packed DEET."

On the beach, Cody tore into the duffel bag. Without even removing her pack she dug frantically for the nets. Then the sun broke through and the mosquitoes disappeared. Derek was scratching like crazy, making the bites bleed even more. She decided not to warn him about infection. "Grab another pack," she said instead. "We're heading back."

Derek stopped scratching. "I'm not going."

Cody stared at him. "You can't stay here alone. You don't even know how to put up the tent."

"I'll sleep on the ground. The sleeping bag will be warm enough," he said, then turned abruptly and stomped down the beach. His words clung to the heavy air.

Cody wondered how long she should wait before chasing after him. "Stubborn," she whispered angrily. "Just like Patterson." Thinking about her brother felt like an added weight in her pack. She dropped onto the drab green mound of duffels and let the pack slip from her shoulders.

Since her parents' divorce three years before, Cody had only seen Patterson one or two weekends a month and on some holidays. The judge had let them each decide who they wanted to live with. Patterson had picked Dad. Cody didn't understand it. Wasn't the divorce bad enough? *Divorce*, as in to dissolve or cut off. She'd looked it up in the dictionary. Her mother never used the word *divorce*. She always said, "We split up." Cody thought that sounded just as bad, like a chicken being split in two.

Cody felt as if she'd been divorced from her brother too. Brief chats on the phone weren't the same as invading his bedroom and talking for hours. But she couldn't live with her father. She wouldn't even *see* him much, after what he'd done. Mostly only through the sheer curtains in the living room when he dropped off Patterson. Telephone conversations were short and to the point. She just answered his questions, which were mostly about school.

Poor Mom, Cody thought miserably, she'd never had a job outside their home. Never cashed a paycheck or balanced a checkbook.

Cody wondered how *wife and mother* looked on a job application. It must have looked all right to the owners of Yakutat Tavern, where her mother was hired. Mostly Mrs. Lewis fixed sandwiches for the visiting fishermen and poured beer. Whipped up supper in the evenings, and listened. Sometimes, she said, she felt more like a psychiatrist than a tavern manager.

Cody jumped, startled by the sound of leaves rustling behind her. "Derek?" She tried looking beyond the trees into the dense forest. Nothing. *Don't freak out*, she told herself. "Derek?"

Farther down the beach, the shiny white bark on a band of dead trees stood as a vivid contrast to an understory of dwarf dogwood and bog orchids. It was hard to remember that this inlet was filled with water from the Pacific Ocean until she spotted a pile of mussel and barnacle shells. Probably an otter's dinner . . . though sometimes bears picked at shellfish during low tide.

Cody shuddered, wondering for a moment if that sound in the trees might be a fifteen-hundred-pound grizzly with razor-sharp claws. But she knew they preferred salmon to people. On trips with the outfitters she'd never seen a bear. Not one. In fact, the only bear she'd ever seen had been raiding the Dumpster behind the tavern.

Still, she snatched the bear horn from the duffel, all set to trigger the siren at the first glimpse of fur. "Derek? If this is a joke I'm not laughing. I'm going to put the kayaks together. Come on, I need help." She decided to let him paddle around for a couple of hours; then he'd wear himself out and want to go back to the lodge. Without socks his feet would be frozen in no time.

She studied the shore for signs of Derek. Still nothing.

Cody pushed a tangle of copper hair off her face. Mosquitoes had attacked her through the dense dance tights. She kicked off her rubber boots and peeled down her muddy socks. The drizzle for which Southeast Alaska was famous would eventually rinse her feet.

"I'm not mad," she hollered, using a new strategy. And she wasn't, either. She just sat on the lumpy canvas, scratched her mosquito bites, and worried about her cousin.

2

hirty minutes had passed since she'd seen him. Where was the little varmint? "Derek!"

She suddenly felt guilty, remembering her aunt's words that morning when she had pulled Cody aside: "I know you'll take good care of Derek." Derek was the youngest of four boys and his mother was overprotective. "Don't tell him I said anything, okay?" Aunt Jessie had said, adding a conspiratorial wink.

Nothing has happened to him, Cody finally decided. If a bear had attacked, she would have heard his screams. Ditto for a moose attack. People still talked about the 1985 Iditarod when Susan Butcher's sled dogs had been ambushed by a pregnant moose. One of her dogs had been stamped to death. Another had died of internal injuries after being kicked up against a tree.

No, she thought, *he's just being stubborn.*

Cody pulled the bag of trail mix from a small zippered pouch marked SNACKS. She picked out the almonds and left the dried peas. She'd just started on the dried coconut when Derek appeared down the beach. He was dragging a long piece of driftwood.

"Where have you been?" she called. "What are you doing with that?"

"I'm going to build a raft."

Cody figured he hadn't heard her hollering earlier. "That's ridiculous," she said, laughing.

"No one in my school has ever seen a glacier." Blood from Derek's mosquito bites had soaked through his T-shirt and mixed with sweat and drizzle, making huge bright pink splotches. He looked as if he'd just returned from a war zone. "I'm going to be the first if it kills me."

Cody remembered the first time she'd seen Hubbard Glacier, a 350-foot-high wall of jagged blue ice rising out of the water. A chunk the size of a skyscraper had broken off and crashed into the water, making waves high enough to surf on. She'd stopped paddling, just bobbing on the rolling surf and staring wide-eyed. Tears had run down her cheeks and she hadn't bothered to wipe them away.

She wasn't about to tell Derek about Hubbard. Then he'd want to paddle all the way down the length of the fjord to get to it. Which was more than a week's journey if the weather held.

Cody tossed him a mosquito net. "I'll get the DEET," she said. "Sometimes I think the little suckers like it." She handed him the trail mix and dug around for the insect repellent. "Tell you what, we can still go to some of the smaller glaciers. We'll camp one night instead of two. Okay?" The compromise sounded reasonable, though she still felt uneasy. Maybe the rustling in the trees had bothered her more than she thought. With the outfitters, she never worried about bears. But they always packed a bear horn *and* a rifle.

"But I want to see Hubbard Glacier." Derek sounded more like a two-year-old than a twelve-year-old. "It's the largest tidewater glacier in North America. Did you know that?"

Cody came up with the first-aid kit. Of course she knew it. "It's too far, Derek, even if we had enough food and supplies. Our parents are only in Juneau for the weekend, remember. One night, that's the deal." Her tone made it clear that this was a take-it-or-leave-it proposition.

Derek stared down at his pitiful piece of driftwood. "Okay."

Working together, they quickly snapped the wooden frames of the kayaks in place. Heavy sky-blue canvas covers fit tightly over the shells. "We'll load the gear after the kayaks are in the water," Cody said. She pulled her wild curls through the back of her No Fear baseball cap—a gift from Patterson—to keep her hair out of her eyes. Then she lifted the bow of her kayak and scooted the long body over the coarse sand.

Even though the kayaks were made for two people, Cody and Derek each had their own. It was still a trick to pack all the gear and leave enough room for feet. Cody unrolled her sleeping bag and tucked it over the wooden seat to cushion her behind. Derek did the same.

Getting in without tipping wasn't easy, but they managed with little water seeping over the sides.

When they had their paddles in hand, it was time to take off. Out on the fjord the wind whipped salt water into whitecaps and the mosquitoes vanished.

"Guess what?" Derek took off his green net, stuffed it in his pocket, then put on his sunglasses. "I can breathe without swallowing a winged snack."

Cody smiled. "Pure protein." She touched her pocket and realized she'd left her shades in the cabin. *Darn.* She rubbed sunscreen on her fair skin then turned to Derek, who slapped at the water as if he were killing flies. "Use the skinny side to cut the water, not the flat side. Or you'll wear yourself out."

Derek wasn't listening. He was taking in the surrounding landscape. "I thought these were the highest mountains in the world."

"The highest *coastal* mountain range in the world," she reminded him. "It's called the Saint Elias Range."

From where Cody was paddling, the fjord looked more like a lake than like part of the mighty Pacific Ocean. She slipped into an easy rhythm, using her upper body. Pushing one arm, pulling the other. Push, pull. Push, pull. No effort. She picked up speed when she glided into an eddy not far from shore.

The water was icy cold, because of the hundreds of glaciers melting and running into the fjord. It was a bone-chilling cold she didn't remember from earlier trips. Of course it was late summer now. The air already whispered a hint of a fall that would pass quickly, just an introduction to breath-stealing winter.

Click, click, click. The water played a tune on the

thousands of mussels and barnacles clinging to the rocks along the shoreline. And to think, she and her brother used to order steamed mussels in restaurants! It was hard to believe she'd actually eaten them, sucking the rubbery blobs out of the shells.

She smiled, wondering what Patterson would think if he saw her now, paddling a kayak in the Alaskan wilderness with their city-slicker cousin. Patterson, who snipped the plastic windows out of bills before putting the envelopes in the paper-recycling bin. Patterson, who dried the kitchen sponge in the toaster. Patterson, who shelved his books alphabetically by the main character's last name.

Cody pushed into the middle of the fjord, grasped the paddle, and stared at the patch of blue sky—much bluer than a California sky. Tilting her head back, she let the sun wash over her. Without socks her toes were half numb, but she didn't care. She was happy she'd decided to stay overnight. Derek would never forget this.

Her kayak hit a series of ripples in the water and she paddled faster, putting her back into each stroke. The faster she paddled, the more invigorated she felt. A slight breeze had sprung up and whitecaps crashed on the bow, sprinkling her with salt.

A seagull dropped a mussel on the rocks, then swooped down and gobbled the meat from the broken shell. Another gull squawked and circled Cody's kayak. It must have had a nest somewhere onshore, with late-season chicks.

Cody paddled even faster now. Each breath kept time with the rhythm of her strokes. She was high on the adrenaline pulsing through her veins.

"Wait up!" Derek called from behind. "You have the food bag!"

Cody lifted her paddle, watching water roll off the blade. Coasting, she made a half circle. Derek was a dot the size of a surf scoter. She hadn't meant to leave him so far behind.

She waited for him to catch up. She sliced a couple of bagels with her Swiss Army knife and slathered them with cream cheese. Smoked salmon was the topper.

Smoked salmon, she thought as she eyed the bright pink flesh. Her friends back home would be inhaling cheeseburgers and pizza. In ten days she would be back in school in Bakersfield, California, wishing she were in Yakutat.

At first she had hated the idea of spending summers in Alaska, away from her friends. Especially when she'd found out her mother had taken a job in a tavern. Now she dreaded going back. Her friends only half listened to her stories. The boys and clothes they talked about seemed so superficial. Now, Cody realized, she was more at home in a tavern than a mall.

In two and a half months of working in Yakutat, her mother made enough money in tips to support the two of them for the rest of the year, along with Dad's child support. Fishermen from all over the world came to Yakutat and spent a small fortune to catch steelhead and king salmon. After a successful fishing trip and an ice chest full of fillets they often tipped five dollars for a single bottle of beer.

"Save some for me." Derek bumped into both her kayak and her thoughts. "I could eat a moose," he said, laying his hand on a bagel.

The drizzle turned into steady rain. Cody slipped her yellow slicker over her life vest, pulled the hood over No Fear, and snapped down the rubber skirt on the kayak. Even a soggy sandwich tasted great in the wild.

"Wash the salmon off your hands when you're done," she said. "You don't want to smell like a grizzly's favorite meal."

Derek stuck his rain-splattered sunglasses in his pocket. "That's a joke, right?"

"No one jokes about grizzly bears in Alaska."

Derek made another bagel and cream cheese sandwich without salmon. "What did you do with the bear horn?"

"It's behind my seat," she said, "and I packed extra batteries."

"We should have brought a horn for me too."

Cody noticed a tangle of twigs bobbing in the distant water. Probably a snag washed into the fjord on the rising tide. As it moved closer she felt a twinge in her backbone. "Derek," she whispered harshly. "Don't move."

"What is it?"

The current seized her kayak and spun it around. Over her shoulder she watched the twigs turn into a fin, a large triangular appendage moving up behind Derek's craft. "Hold still," she hissed over the wind as the current tried to pull them apart. Until now she hadn't realized how swift the current was that day. The water tumbling down the mountains from rivers and glaciers must have added a powerful tug to the tides.

"What's wrong?" he whispered again.

Cody silently pointed to the dorsal fin less than twenty yards out, speeding toward the kayaks. "I think it's a shark."

Even in the cold wind Derek's cheeks lost all their redness. They drained to the color of the snowcapped peaks. He gripped his paddle, turning his knuckles the same stark white. Then he stared at the fin closing in on him. "How did it get in here?"

"This is the ocean." Her matter-of-fact statement was lost on the brisk breeze. *It must have come in at Disenchantment Bay*, she meant to add. *Near Hubbard*. But she couldn't get the words out.

"What're we going to do?" Derek looked as if he was about to heave his sandwich. "Should we throw it some salmon?"

"You want to chum it?" Cody stared unblinkingly as the fin made a wide circle. If she whacked the side of her kayak with her paddle, the noise might scare it away. Or it might make it mad, make it want to attack.

Derek shivered. Then he started scratching his forehead, triggering a series of tiny red pools. "Can we outrun it?"

The creature made another pass and this time she noted the curved dorsal fin. "This was your idea, cousin dear," she said, and used her paddle to shove his kayak toward the fin. "Shark bait!"

"Stop it!" he screamed. "What are you doing?"

Cody burst out laughing. "It isn't a shark, stupid. It's a white-sided dolphin."

It took a few seconds for her words to sink in. When they did, Derek threw a soggy bagel at her. "I'll get you for this!" he shouted.

"First you have to catch me!" Cody shot back. "It serves you right for making me wait on the beach." She was already pushing her paddle through the choppy water.

3

hen the sun peeked through the dreary clouds Cody shed her slicker and tied it to her paddle. The makeshift sail swelled under the chilling wind blowing off the ice-capped mountains. Still, she was sweaty.

Southeast Alaska was one of those weird places where the tips of your ears could be crisp-fried to a crackling crunch while your toes were frozen to the point of tissue destruction. It seemed as if everyone who spent time here was frostbitten sooner or later. Fingers, toes, or cheeks.

She unsnapped the rubber skirt and rolled it back. Sweat, she knew, could freeze, like any kind of water. Some natives used the freeze-dried method for drying laundry: They'd hang wet clothes outside and let them freeze. Then they'd shake out the frozen water, leaving the clothes ready to wear.

Cody lowered her sail and glided into a narrow channel. The sandy shores were lost to a corridor of guano-splashed rock. She stared up at steep cliffs that rose so high that the sky was only a thin gray stripe far above. Raw peaks cut into cotton-ball clouds.

The current moved faster here, a torrent of water

that twisted and rolled past cliffs dotted with empty swallow's nests. It seemed more like a river than an inlet of seawater. She half expected rapids to bubble up around the next bend, but that was ridiculous.

Cody paddled hard to keep from hitting the steep walls, but closer and closer she rolled toward the murky water slapping the granite. Both rock and water had minds of their own. Two against one. No fair.

Somehow she didn't remember the current being this treacherous. The other times she'd paddled this canyon there'd been another person in her kayak. Two against two. Those were much better odds.

Her muscles screamed as she backpaddled feverishly, just missing a jagged rock aimed at her head. Finally the narrow corridor spit her out. On the other side, her kayak floated freely into clean waters rimmed with sandy beaches. She drew in a deep breath, and her pulse steadied to a more normal rhythm.

As the sun continued to drop, the sky turned a deep metallic gray, almost the color of the pickup, now sitting in the clump of berry vines. Cody glanced at her watch. Eight o'clock. Time to make camp. They shouldn't tread any deeper into the fjord. Tomorrow they'd have to paddle all the way back.

She knew that finding a good campsite could be tricky; tides sometimes fluctuated twenty-five feet a day in Southeast Alaska, so beaches and meadows that looked inviting might be flooded within hours.

Worry poked at her as she pictured Derek in the narrow canyon. "Derek?" she called. Coasting with most of her body below the waterline, she felt like one of the tide-pool creatures. Soon she and Derek would pitch their tent and sleep in the splash zone.

"Ya-hoo!" The words echoed from the canyon, and she smiled.

Cody laid her paddle across her lap and rubbed the back of her neck. Derek's hands were probably as sore as a bad tooth by now. She'd had blisters on her hands after her first day in a kayak. Now her palms were callused, from chopping kindling and other chores at the tavern.

She pointed the nose of her kayak at a protected cove, one of the overnight spots used by the outfitters. Gliding into the shallow water, she stuck her paddle in the sand and steadied her craft. Thank goodness for rubber boots, she thought, stepping into the white foam curling out from shore. Rubber boots with their waffle soles were good on sloppy ground; on sunny days she turned them down to her ankles.

After dragging the kayak above the waterline, she unwound the bow rope and wrapped it around a tree stump. "Over here!" she called to Derek a few minutes later.

Derek waved back and paddled to shore. "That was so cool! I almost flipped a dozen times!" His soft dark hair tumbled childlike over his forehead, making him look about six years old. "Do we go back that way?"

"How else would we get back?"

He climbed stiffly out of his kayak, almost tipping it over. "Why can't we camp on the other shore? Closer to those glaciers?" he asked, picking at the shiny white blister on his hand. "I thought glaciers flowed into the water, then chunks of ice broke off and fell in."

"It's called calving, Derek. But only tidewater glaciers touch the water and calve. These are hanging glaciers." Cody glanced across the fjord at the silver lines of ice striping the mountains, knowing that nameless glaciers had scoured the bases of these peaks for centuries. "If we were on the same side, we wouldn't be able to see them at all," she said, shrugging out of her life vest. "We'd be underneath them and the trees would be in the way."

Derek tied his bowline, then dropped onto the deep sand and stared at the frozen rivers. Each time the sun broke through, the glaciers shone like satin ribbons. "Awesome," he said softly.

"Yeah." She dropped next to him and flipped through her tide table. "We have to drag the kayaks above the high-tide line."

"I can't get used to it," he said. "This water looks more like a lake."

"Weird, huh?"

It seemed to take forever to clear a flat spot for the orange dome tent. Turning their arms into shovels and rakes, they rid a sandy circle of driftwood and rocks, then tossed sleeping bags inside the tent, along with personal gear. The kitchen stuff was piled as far away as possible from the tents, near the kayaks, which had been dragged above the high-tide line earlier.

Cody hooked the bear horn over her belt and

grabbed her washcloth and soap. Then she thought twice and tossed Derek the horn. "We'll start dinner when I get back." She felt stiff as she teetered across a fallen tree, as if her joints had started to freeze. "I'm going to the falls to wash up."

She jumped down on the far side of the log and headed up a wide trail that snaked into the rain forest. Although it was after nine at night, it would stay light for several hours. But inside the forest, tall trees with dense canopies pulled everything into inky shadows. Tangled vines and dead limbs twisted overhead. Some bird she couldn't name screeched at her for trespassing.

Cody belted out her favorite Alaskan ballad in case there were any bears around. If they heard you coming, they got out of the way. That was what the outfitters told their clients. At times like this she liked to think of their Latin name, *Ursus arctos horribilis*.

After a quarter of a mile, the trail broke out of the woods and opened up to a stream that rushed down from a series of waterfalls. Indian paintbrush and blue-pod lupine studded the few dry patches. They were similar to the wildflowers in California but a lot taller, probably because of Alaska's longer summer days. Fish swam in a pool under the falls, looking huge from the water's magnification. Too bad she hadn't packed her fishing gear. Nothing tasted better than fresh fish cooked over an open fire.

Cody hesitated a minute before stripping to her waist. She suddenly had the uneasy feeling that someone was watching her from deep in the forest. *Ridiculous*, she chided herself.

The sun ducked behind a mountain with a finality that made her even more restless. She wasn't afraid of the dark, so that wasn't it. It was something else. Something she didn't want to name. She shivered.

Keeping her sports bra on, she lathered her armpits. She soaked her washcloth, which was so icy cold it numbed the tips of her fingers. She washed her face and rinsed her pits, then let the breeze raise goose bumps on her skin.

That was when she heard it: rustling in the bushes. On the other side of the stream. Startled, she turned. "Derek?" Nothing. Then more rustling. "Derek?" Maybe he wanted to pay her back for joking about the shark? But the noise was coming from upstream, not down.

Cody scrambled up on a boulder and scanned the trees. But the bushy vines and limbs guarded the forest against her scrutiny.

While she was straining to see, her boot slipped on something squishy. She looked down: bear scat. It was fresh, too. Black bear or grizzly? She didn't know.

Calm. Stay calm, she told herself. *Don't panic. Animals can smell fear. And I probably stink with it.*

Stupid! Only bears would make such a wide trail through the forest. Nothing else. Cody wanted to race back to the beach, grab her kayak, and split. But she knew better. Running brought out the hunting instinct in predators. She would instantly become prey.

A black bear suddenly pushed into the sunlight across the stream. Cody didn't move. Not a single eyelash. The bear looked at her, surprised. She looked back, but not directly into his eyes.

I'm not a threat, she willed to the animal across the water.

If it made a move at her, she would turn sideways. Raise her arms. Make herself look taller. Bigger. Meaner.

All these thoughts rushed through her head in seconds. And then: *If it doesn't act aggressive, I'll stand still until it leaves.*

Neither one of them moved.

Even from across the water she could smell its foul breath. It smelled as if it had recently eaten something dead. Its fur was a matted mess—nothing like a bear in a zoo. This bear was wild in a way she couldn't describe.

Then another sound of rustling in the trees, even louder than before. The noise was behind the bear and farther upstream. Maybe the bear had a mate. Or worse, maybe it had cubs. Mother bears were known to rip people apart if they thought their cubs were threatened.

Suddenly the bear dropped to all fours and left the clearing as quickly as it had appeared. Only when the sounds of trampled branches faded far into the forest did Cody let out her breath, a sigh of relief that was almost a sob. Then she started back down the trail. Her steps were painfully slow because she was walking backward. She didn't want the bear to think she was running away. She felt as if its eyes were burning holes in her T-shirt.

Back in camp, Derek had unwrapped the food for dinner and spread it out on a tarp. All he needed was a sign saying BEAR OPEN HOUSE, Cody thought. The bear horn was twenty yards away on a rock. Cody didn't have the energy for a lecture. Instead she made a silent vow to stick together until they returned to Yakutat. She never should have left him alone in camp in the first place.

"Since we're going back a day early, can we eat tomorrow night's dinner too?" A pot of water was boiling on the single burner. Derek ripped the package of macaroni with his teeth. "It'll make the kayaks lighter."

She nodded. "Sure," she said, not really listening.

Cody clipped the bear horn on. There was no reason to tell him she had seen a bear at the waterfall. Then neither of them would get any sleep. Maybe she would tell him tomorrow on their way back to the lodge. He would be relieved they were heading back a day early.

Cody loaded the rest of the food bags into her kayak and tucked her life vest tightly over them while Derek worked on dinner. She checked the bow rope to make sure it was secured to the tree stump, then sprayed a ring of Lysol around the kayak—a trick the outfitters used to mask the smell of food. She sprayed a thick ring around the tent too, just to be safe.

After dinner Cody washed the cooking utensils,

using sand to scrape off bits of food and grease and put them in her kayak. She added more wood to the fire and scooted closer to the flames. But no matter how close she sat, she couldn't warm up.

Why had the bear turned and split like that? She thought about the other noise she'd heard. Whatever it was, it probably had saved her life.

After half an hour she couldn't see more than fifteen or twenty feet beyond the fire. And past the circle of light the blackness was complete. Derek poked at the coals with a twig, and sparks danced in the air. Ash floated on the chilling breeze.

Cold and tired, Cody left the dwindling fire and crawled into the tent. She stuck the bear horn in one boot, her flashlight in the other. Both boots were pressed up against her side so that she could find them in the dark. Then she wormed into her bag, shivering as her feet slid over the cool nylon.

Derek crawled into the tent behind her and arranged his boots for a pillow. "This is so cool."

Cody wished she'd thought of using her life vest for a pillow. But it was in the kayak and she didn't have the energy to get it.

"Too bad I can't spend every summer in Alaska," Derek said from inside his sleeping bag. "But my mom would never let me."

"She might if my mom talked to her."

There was a long silence between them. Cody figured Derek had gone to sleep. She listened to the wind rustle the leaves and worried that the bear might smell the macaroni and cheese.

Bears were amazing sniffers. The news was full of reports of grizzlies ripping into vans and cars. They could smell a stick of gum in a closed car trunk.

"Cody?"

Cody nearly jumped out of her sleeping bag. "Geez, Derek. You scared me to death. I thought you were asleep."

"Can I ask you something?"

She caught her breath. "Sure."

"What happened with your mom and dad? The divorce and stuff?"

Cody wished she had a pillow to punch. She'd asked herself that question a thousand times. "It was Dad's fault," she said, surprised she'd blurted it out like that. "But I don't want to talk about it."

"You're not mad, are you?"

Yeah, she was mad. But not at him. "No, I'm not mad. Go to sleep."

Soon the silence grew into a sound of its own—a dull throbbing in her ears—until the rumble of Derek's snoring took over.

Cody was totally exhausted but her mind wouldn't shut down. The whole family was probably still talking about the divorce. Dad and the other woman, who was only twenty-five. Now they all lived together: her father, her brother, and Tonya, the stepmother. One big happy family. It was enough to make you puke.

Back then, her mother had stared at the TV—the one-eyed monster, she called it—in a kind of shock. Her mind, her heart, everything had refused to accept what was happening. The waiting—the papers demanding signatures, more papers—the uncertainties about their future.

Cody had missed several days of school, and when she had gone back, she hadn't been able to concentrate. She'd sit for hours staring at her open notebook—the words blurred and meaningless, replaying the day her father told her, "I'm so sorry, Cody. Your mother and I tried to work it out." Then the piercing words "I'm leaving."

The following weeks stretched into months, empty days piling up like old newspapers. No movies with her friends, no hanging out at the mall, no sleepovers. Later the focus shifted to staying busy by cleaning. She'd used every attachment on the vacuum cleaner, sucking dust off baseboards, window frames, even upholstered chairs. Mostly it was just a lot of noise; it didn't even begin to fill the void left by Dad and Patterson.

Cody hated her father for what he had done. She'd never forgive him.

4

t first Cody didn't think she'd been asleep. But she awakened startled and realized she'd been having one of her nightmares about the divorce. Her parents' voices had been calm and low. Maybe that was what was so scary. Neat and clean, like folding laundry. Orderly piles stacked and ready to be put away. Patterson in the Dad dresser. Cody in the Mom drawer.

Girlfriend. The word fit Tonya. At least the *girl* part. One of her dad's students at the university. *Stepmother.* Cody secretly called her *step-monster.* A small wedding only a month after the divorce. "To satisfy the court." Dad had said it like an apology. "Because Patterson is going to live with us."

Even now Cody could hear her mother's sobs, could see the strained question on her lips. "I don't understand," she'd kept repeating, not fully aware of what was happening. Cody hadn't been able to stand the hurt in her mother's voice.

Cody shivered, realizing that the foot of her sleeping bag was wet. Water had even soaked that end of the foam pad underneath. "Darn," she scolded herself, grabbing her flashlight. "Wake up." She poked Derek. "We have to move the tent."

"Huh?"

"Where's your flashlight?" she said, slipping into her cold boots. "Put on your boots."

It was dangerous to be wet, especially if a chill set in. Body temperature would drop as blood abandoned fingers and toes to warm the vital organs. That was how frostbite started, with the destruction of skin and underlying tissue. She didn't want to think about what happened next.

Cody unzipped the tent flap and crawled partway into the vestibule. The beam of her flashlight shone on the water there. Cautiously she touched the water. It was colder than she'd expected: a dull, bitter cold.

The water was slowly seeping higher. So slowly that she could barely see it move. "I messed up with the tide," she said. "We have to pull the stakes and move the tent."

"With everything in it?" Derek asked from inside.

"We can drag it to higher ground."

Her toes felt like shriveled-up prunes inside her boots. She didn't have dry socks. Derek didn't have any socks. The sun wouldn't be up for several more hours and might not even break through the clouds when it did rise.

Cody pulled up the stakes on one side of the tent. Derek uprooted those on the other side. They dragged the tent up the sandy slope to the thick underbrush encroaching on the beach. "The tent should have been up here against the bushes in the first place," she said, straining to catch her breath. "I can't believe it. I must have looked at the wrong date in the tide book. How could I have been so stupid?"

"I still don't get it," Derek said. "How did the water come into the tent?"

Cody reminded him yet again that the fjord was filled from the ocean. "I misread the tide table," she repeated dully. "Pretty soon the water will go back out, moving to low tide."

"Right," he mumbled.

With the tent restaked they crawled back inside, pushing into their sleeping bags. Cody kept to the head end of hers, which was still dry. "We'll rebuild the fire in the morning," she said, rubbing her shriveled toes. With a bit of maneuvering she could pull the sleeves of her sweatshirt over her cold feet. "Have a hot breakfast and thaw out."

Cody knew Derek had nodded off because his dull snores cut through the air. Her cousin could sleep anywhere, just like Patterson. She curled into a warm ball and pictured a campfire on the beach—red hot and crackling with driftwood. Her hands were wrapped around a mug of steamy cocoa topped with marshmallows. A skillet of bacon was sizzling next to a griddle full of salmonberry hotcakes.

She was warmer now, dreaming of a cloudless sky. No drizzle or mist, just enough of a breeze to keep the mosquitoes away. Then a tidal wave crashed on the campfire. Everything was drenched. Hotcakes and bacon. Even her mug of cocoa.

Cody woke up, startled.

She grabbed her flashlight. Water was still seeping into the tent. Something was wrong. *Really* wrong. She would wake Derek, but then what? This couldn't be the tide; it had to be something else. She tried to think of a logical explanation, a reason why the water was still rising.

What? Nothing came to her.

"Derek?" She tried to hide the urgency in her voice. "Wake up."

"Now what?"

Fortunately the daypacks were at the high end of the tent and still dry. "Something's wrong." She peeled the wet sweatshirt from her feet. Her toes had turned from prunes to Popsicles. She rubbed them briskly. "The water is still rising."

Derek scooted back, focusing his beam of light on the foot of the tent. "The tide?"

She shook her head. "The tide doesn't come up this high."

"Never?" he asked.

"Never."

The dial on her watch showed it was 3:00 A.M. It would start getting light in another hour. There was nothing she could do in the dark. "We have to stay awake till morning."

Derek snatched the last of his dry clothes from his pack. "What do you think it is?"

"I don't know."

"Are you scared?"

"No," she lied.

Cody checked the water level every ten minutes for the next hour. She marked the water's progress with an extra tent stake. They squatted in their boots, inching backward as the water seeped higher. Soon they were shoved against the back of the tent.

"What happened to low tide?" Derek asked, shivering.

Cody didn't answer. She was transfixed by the early-morning light as it turned the nylon dome into a bright orange ball. "At least the sun's out."

Derek followed Cody out of the tent into six inches of water. She stopped, staring at the strange surroundings. The water in the fjord had turned a weird color. Not the usual salty blue-green but almost clear, as if it was covered with a layer of fresh water.

In some places the water had begun invading the forest. The roots of trees and vines normally far above the high-tide line were now drowning. The eeriest thing of all was the quiet.

Cody quickly yanked the tent stakes from the waterlogged ground. They piled what they had in the tent in a soggy heap; then Cody went to get her kayak.

"We'll be safe on the water," she said, wading in the direction of her kayak. "If we paddle fast enough we'll be on the beach we launched from before it's time for lunch. How're the blisters on your hands?"

Cody didn't listen for his answer. She was too busy worrying about what the beach they had taken off from would look like when they got back. Would there be any beach left? Or would it be flooded? And if so, how would they unload? Unloading the kayaks in water would be hard enough; wading through water while loaded down with gear would be impossible.

Cody stopped in her watery tracks. Her kayak had been tied to a stump on the beach twenty feet above the high-tide line. "I don't believe it." She heard the panic in her voice.

The stump was completely covered by clear icy water. Her kayak was drifting in the middle of the fjord, overturned. The stove and fuel had probably sunk as soon as the kayak capsized. Food bags and other supplies floated in the water near the bow.

A breeze whipped off the ice, cutting through Cody's clothes. She stood shaking as her life vest bobbed a final farewell, a bright orange SOS on the rising tide. Within seconds the kayak and vest disappeared around the bend on their way toward Hubbard Glacier.

Cody and Derek exchanged frightened glances. A strained silence hung between them like an invisible hull over their drowning camp.

5

Cody stood ankle deep in the clear water, wobbling slightly as shock waves hit her. Kayak lost. No food. No life vest. Derek opened his mouth and gasped in the icy air. He didn't say anything either. Their lack of words was a hundred times more deafening than if they'd screamed.

The bright sun burned through a flawless blue sky. It was actually hot, which was unusual in Southeast Alaska. The water had become like a magnifying glass, sending prisms bouncing across the fjord. Each beam was blinding in its brilliance. Blinding and burning.

Cody squinted. No sunglasses. No sunscreen. She couldn't believe she'd left her shades behind.

Derek asked the obvious question: "Shouldn't we go after it?"

Cody stood still, torn by the desire to rescue her kayak and the knowledge that she couldn't swim after it. There was no chance to run it down in Derek's kayak. Without the weight of people and gear, it was moving much too swiftly. She simply stood on the rock with water lapping her boots, gazing in the direction where her kayak had disappeared.

"We'd never catch it," she said.

Cody raked her fingers through her hair, snagging a broken nail in her tangled curls. She slipped on No Fear and adjusted the brim to shade her eyes. "Where's the extra paddle?"

"I think it's in my kayak."

"I hope you're right."

With only one paddle it would be nearly impossible to maneuver two people through the water. She held her breath and mentally crossed her fingers, then looked inside Derek's kayak. There it was—in all its varnished glory—clamped safely inside.

It's more than just a paddle, she thought as she touched the smooth wood. *With two paddles we can make it. We have to.*

Derek pulled the bag of trail mix from inside his shirt. "I'm starving."

She stared at him. "Was that in the tent?"

Derek nodded. "Midnight snack."

Cody couldn't decide if she should hug him or slug him. All the food, even the nonfood smelly stuff like toothpaste and sunscreen, had been stowed in her kayak.

Derek had watched her circle the kayak spraying Lysol. He'd even asked her about it. No food within fifty feet of our tent, she'd told him, bears are amazing sniffers.

The irony of it made her laugh so hard that tears filled her eyes. She quickly wiped them away, not wanting to add another drop to the already soggy surroundings.

Then she swore—not at Derek, but at the situation—using the one word she never said aloud. She felt a lot better.

"Let's hurry up and get loaded," she said. "You carry the rest of the stuff down here and I'll pack it up."

Cody straddled the bow and made a mental inventory of the remaining gear: one kayak, two paddles, one tent (wet), one life vest, two sleeping bags (wet), two flashlights, two water bottles (one empty, one half full), one cooking pot, one bear horn, matches inside a plastic bag, and clothes.

Just as quickly she counted what they'd lost: one kayak, one paddle, one life vest, stove and fuel, the other cooking pot, water purifier, extra batteries, plus the smelly stuff like sunscreen, insect repellent, first-aid ointment, and Lysol. All the food, except a small bag of trail mix.

Cody tossed the tent sack in front, climbed in, and shoved it forward with her feet. Personal gear came next. The wet sleeping bags were draped over the two seats. They'd dry in no time in this heat. She wondered what had happened to all the mosquitoes and seagulls.

She finished packing while concentrating on the gurgling noise coming from the trees along the shore. The carbon dioxide–breathing plants were suffocating in the rising water. Who would have thought that trees would cry out when they were drowning?

Cody pushed a sweaty strand of hair under No Fear and looked at Derek. He was building two piles of trail mix on a rock, counting out equal numbers of almonds and raisins and dried peas.

"We're not shipwrecked, you know, and we won't be on this beach forever." Cody tossed him the lone life vest. "You wear it."

"Why me?"

"I'm the captain and what I say goes."

Derek sighed long and loud. He knew better than to argue with her. He'd never win anyway. He just grabbed a paddle and took his place in back. He knew without being told that his captain-cousin would demand the front seat.

Out on the water, the eight-foot craft glided easily up the fjord toward Yakutat. But the air was so hot and thick that it was difficult to take in. Cody tied a damp bandanna over her nose and mouth, and breathing became easier. Then she pulled some of her hair loose so that it covered her ears. Derek's ears were probably already sunburned.

"Thank goodness we're not on a sailboat," she said, worrying why there wasn't the slightest hint of a breeze. In the back of her mind the phrase *calm before the storm* repeated itself.

An unspoken question prodded her into the narrow seawater passage. They hadn't mentioned the rising water since early this morning. The water level was coming up even faster now.

She felt as if she were inside a small fishbowl. Someone was carrying the bowl and water was sloshing up the glass sides, threatening to spill out. But the sides of this bowl were rugged mountains of record height, Mount Saint Elias on the north, Mount Fairweather on the south. Both stood in ranges thick with impenetrable forests of western hemlock and Sitka spruce. And glaciers, such a mass of frozen rivers most of them didn't have names.

Cody's shoulders started throbbing with a dull ache that pulled at her muscles. She set the paddle across her lap for a minute and watched water drip off the blade. Without sunglasses she couldn't look at them too long; the drops were blinding in the bright sun.

She lifted the corner of her bandanna and took a single satisfying tug on her water bottle. The water felt cool in her dry throat and helped fill the void in her stomach. Last night's macaroni and cheese was long gone. Trail mix tasted like gravel in the heat and made her thirsty. Being in a kayak surrounded by water they knew they couldn't drink made most people wolfishly thirsty.

"It's like we're in a swimming pool," Derek said. "Someone is filling it with a fat hose cranked up full blast. And it's gonna overflow if someone doesn't turn it off."

Derek had read her mind again, picked up on her thoughts about the fishbowl. She hated it when he did that. Patterson did it too.

Well, she couldn't tell someone to pull the plug.

Cody's light strokes were suddenly challenged by a strong current, and she dug her paddle in deeper. "Push!" she shouted back. "Harder!"

It felt as if some invisible force were pulling them backward, away from Yakutat. She concentrated on deep even strokes. Push, pull. Even breathing. In, out. Even, steady. Push, pull. Breathing timed with strokes. Derek followed her lead.

The bandanna slipped from her face. She didn't stop to retie it. Sweat dripped into her eyes. She blinked away the stinging salt. The paddle was slick with sweat and water. Like wet feet, wet hands caused blisters. She sacrificed a few seconds to wrap her sweatshirt around the slippery handle.

She figured that the current should have been pushing them forward, in the direction of Yakutat and the beach near the boggy trail that climbed uphill to the pickup. Instead, it was fighting them. Then she realized that all the beaches were buried in a watery grave, as the shoreline plants were. They'd probably have to swim through the forest to the truck.

The Tide: that was how Cody thought about it—with a capital letter. It should be receding. Ebb and flow and gravitational pull. She'd studied it in science class. The moon and sun controlled the surface level of oceans, bays, gulfs, inlets, and fjords.

But the water in Russell Fjord was intent on rising, with no signs of slacking off. The current was using all its muscle to fight the two paddlers, pulling on them from the open sea as if it would never let them go.

"We're hardly moving," Derek said. "I've been watching the same clump of trees for half an hour."

Cody studied the mountains and forests through the early-morning glare. A landscape that should have been passing slowly to the side and rear of the kayak, passing behind them as they skimmed forward.

Derek was right: Everything stood in place.

Her tongue stuck to the roof of her mouth and she swallowed hard. She didn't remember the outfitters mentioning a tide that refused to fall.

She thought about the history of the fjord. Eight hundred years ago a massive glacier had filled both Disenchantment Bay and Yakutat Bay and extended into the Pacific Ocean. Russell Fjord had been blocked by a dam of ice and could only drain into the ocean along one channel, called Old Situk Creek.

The answer came as clear as the freshwater layer on top of the seawater.

"I know why the water is still rising," she gasped.

6

"I don't get it," Derek said after she'd explained it. "What do you mean Hubbard surged?"

Cody thought of another word for *surge*. "It advanced." She remembered the outfitters talking about Hubbard Glacier one night after she'd crawled into her tent. They had used simple terms: *advance* and *retreat*. To advance meant to move forward. To retreat meant to move back.

Their conversation came back to her: 1986 was the last time Hubbard Glacier had surged. More than seventy miles long, the river of slowly moving ice had slid across the mouth of Russell Fjord, sealing off Disenchantment Bay and forming the world's largest glacier-formed lake.

"Are you sure?" Derek asked.

"All the streams and rivers are draining into the fjord." She shouted over the wind, which was picking up. "All the water that usually flows out to sea on the tide doesn't have anywhere to go."

"No way out."

She silently finished his thought: *Just like us.*

She gripped her paddle as a fist of wind rumbled down the passage, smacking them in the face. The kayak lunged another foot backward. This wasn't good at all. It was as if Yakutat were intent on pushing them away.

A wind like this usually brought foul weather. An old Alaskan saying jabbed at her: "If you don't like the weather, wait five minutes."

Until now she hadn't fully understood what it meant. But in just the past five minutes the sky, so transparent that you felt you could reach up and touch the sun, had disappeared. *Whammo*, everything had fallen into darkness under bruise-colored clouds.

The wind was driving hard from Yakutat, pushing ahead of a storm like a warning.

Cody handed Derek a rain slicker over her shoulder. She tied the bandanna over No Fear to keep it from blowing off and snapped the rubber skirt around her waist. Earth and water. Now wind. It seemed as if the entire universe were against them.

We can find some kind of shelter, she thought, *even if it's only under a rocky ledge. Tie up and wait out the storm. Then turn around and battle the current back to Yakutat*. That's what she told Derek. But she knew storms like the one coming were unpredictable.

No food. No fresh water pounded at her. And *No one knows we're out here*.

She checked her watch. She knew they wouldn't be missed until Mom and Aunt Jessie returned from Juneau. The plane wasn't due in until the next day, weather permitting. Small planes were grounded during storms.

Her mother wouldn't find the note she'd left—

scrawled on a used envelope and taped to the milk carton inside the fridge so that Derek wouldn't see it—until she came back to the cabin.

Cody turned the kayak around. The wind swirled in minitornados that churned the water and sent it splashing over the bow. The kayak lurched forward in awkward spurts, lifting and falling as it slapped wildly at the uneven swells.

That was when she heard it.

A deafening crash rumbled through the steep mountain corridors. Thunder. She shuddered at the sound. It was too close. And it seemed to be in front of them. It didn't seem possible. All the wind was blowing from behind, chasing them, closing in.

Maybe a second storm was coming at them from the ocean. They could be squashed by two raging storms.

The noise was like a firecracker set off in a tin can. Another bend in the fjord. There were no rocky ledges here either, or secluded coves. There was no shelter of any kind, except a giant tidewater glacier with its snout edging into the water.

"Is that Hubbard?" Derek hollered over the wind.

Cody shook her head. "It can't be." She couldn't believe the massive wall of ice less than a mile away. The frozen face was as long as a football field across and more than ten stories high.

A woeful moan grew into a deafening roar, like the dull static of white noise. It hadn't been thunder after all. A chunk of ice the size of Yakutat Tavern broke loose and plummeted into the water. Seagulls appeared from nowhere, swooping down to feed on the brine shrimp brought up by the turbulence.

"Backpaddle!" Cody shouted.

A series of icy walls of waves four or five feet high rolled out from the broken chunk, now an enormous iceberg bobbing in the salt water. The giant waves aimed at the kayak.

Cody knew she should keep paddling, put as much water as possible between the iceberg and the kayak, but the undercurrent was too strong and much too swift. If the waves slammed the craft just right, her paddle would be torn from her grip.

"Hang on to your paddle!"

The first wave hit them sideways, spraying salt and buckets of water. The kayak dropped into a deep trough, tipped unsteadily, and nearly capsized. It lolled on its side and would have spit them out if it hadn't been for the rubber skirts holding them in. The kayak rolled back the other way and righted itself.

Derek cried, "Here comes another one!"

The second wave struck harder than the first, lifting the kayak and letting it coast on the crest. One, two, three seconds. It seemed like a lifetime. Then it dropped flat into a deep trough. The wooden craft shook when it hit bottom, threatening to split at its canvas shell.

Wave after wave.

Boom, boom, boom.

The next wave sailed right over the bow and slapped Cody in the face. She coughed, unable to catch her breath. She felt as if she were drowning; still in the kayak and above water, but choking instead of taking in oxygen.

Even now the noise wouldn't let up—the relentless gusts, the scream of seagulls, the slapping of paddles—all loud enough to wake the dead.

Cody clung to the paddle as to life itself, shouting to Derek to do the same.

The kayak finally pulled out of the wave and glided into the open air. Cody coughed up seawater. She'd swallowed a ton. Salt scraped the back of her throat.

"You okay?" she called back.

"Yeah," Derek returned weakly.

"Paddle?" she barely managed.

"Got it."

Both paddles still in hand. Two sticks. This crumb of news filled her with hope.

With a death grip she paddled hard on the right to turn the kayak before the next set of waves hit. Being slammed head-on was better than taking a lateral strike. It came, as she'd known it would. *Slam!* Not quite as hard as before. But the kayak still spun like a kicked bottle.

Each time a wave hit the kayak, water seeped into the rubber skirt. Several inches sloshed in the bottom of the craft. Some had even worked its way inside her knee-high boots. Everything was drenched: clothes, gear, and paddlers.

The waves finally weakened, dying into swells less

than a foot high. Cody slumped in her seat; her shoulders sagged. She was utterly exhausted. "We made it."

High above the kayak and less than a half mile away the glacier mirrored a dozen shades of blue. Some of the ice was so light it was nearly colorless; some of it was so dark it looked black. The face of the glacier, where the ice had broken off, wore a new expression now, an ice sculpture of hundred-foot-high spires and turrets.

Catching her breath, she thought about how much of the earth was covered with ice—one-tenth, she'd learned from the outfitters. An entire ocean was covered with it, like a white layer of congealed fat on a pot of cold turkey soup.

She forced herself to put her paddle back in the water. Her muscles screamed at the first stroke. Her shoulder blades felt as if someone were tightening them with screws.

"We have to get away from the glacier," she said. "Before it calves again."

"I can't lift the paddle."

But Derek did. Barely. One stroke, then two.

Soon the kayak skimmed water that spread across the fjord like soluble paints on paper, bleeding colors too mixed up to have their own names. They were alone in this vast maze of land and water and disconnected from everything that was familiar. Everything that was safe.

Cody wished they'd never left Yakutat.

7

The violent tailwind died to an occasional gust, but the undercurrent stayed just as fierce as before, drawing the kayak toward the ocean—toward Disenchantment Bay and Hubbard Glacier.

"Some people think the Ice Age is still with us," Cody said. "That we're in a warmer phase of it."

Derek strained with each stroke. "Do you think that berg is like the one that sank the *Titanic*?"

"That's just a baby," she said. "Some of them are over a hundred miles long."

"No way!"

"*Way*."

Cody looked back at the clouds suspended over Yakutat: a solid wall of black. "Maybe we'll luck out," she said. "Maybe the storm will dump all its rain in town. It's about time we had some *good* luck."

The kayak skimmed away from the calving glacier, away from the three-story iceberg, in case it rolled. "No one in California will believe this," Derek said.

Cody's strokes were as lifeless as her arms, with about as much power as a frayed bow rope. Her shorts and T-shirt were soaked. Her sleeping bag was a soggy mess under her rear. She wondered if wet clothes could freeze to skin.

"If it's raining in Yakutat," Derek asked, "won't all the water drain into the fjord?"

"Add tons of water from rivers and streams and runoff from glaciers," she said.

Cody peeled off her rain slicker, then unsnapped the rubber skirt and rolled it back. Earlier her toes had been numb. Now they'd started to burn. The glare off the ice and water was blinding, like having a sunlamp plugged in only inches from her face.

"Look for a place to tie up." She forced the water away with deep strokes, glancing at Derek. "We have to build a fire and dry out."

Derek pulled his T-shirt away from his wrinkled skin. The whiteness was stark against his tanned arms. "Maybe there's something to eat around here."

"We should be able to find some berries." Cody was half starved too. She had a gnawing sensation that felt as if her stomach had started eating itself. "Where's the trail mix?"

"Buried at sea along with my sunglasses."

"How did that happen?"

"They just fell overboard."

At a cultural fair earlier in the summer Cody had watched natives drying salmon, roasting seal flippers, smoking bear meat, and fermenting fishheads. Now she scanned the terrain above the waterline and wished she could remember how they preserved berries.

She wasn't looking for shelter anymore, just a

small clearing in the trees where water met land. A place to tie the kayak, build a fire, and find something to eat. She scanned the areas that had once been mudflats and sandy beaches, that had supported a world of small animals only the day before, now all under water. Somewhere there had to be a place to stop.

Cody couldn't remember ever being this tired. She was so exhausted that she felt like dropping her head in her hands and blubbering like a baby. Suddenly she was overcome with emotion. *If I don't make it back to Yakutat, and die out here in the wilderness, then Mom will be alone*, she thought.

I'm all Mom has now. We can't die out here.

There was another reason to survive. She'd never told her dad how she felt about what he'd done. She'd written lots of letters but never mailed any of them.

Cody swallowed the ache in her throat, using all her strength to search the old-growth trees and rocky knobs for a place to tie up. Normally grasses and sedges sprinkled the shoreline, mixed with splashes of colorful wildflowers. Edible herbs, even. Now they lay rotting under several feet of water.

She wondered what finally had happened back in 1986, when Hubbard had surged. The glacier hadn't closed off Disenchantment Bay forever; otherwise Russell Fjord would still be a lake. Then she wondered if seals and porpoises had been trapped in here too. If only she'd paid more attention when the outfitters had talked about it.

She blinked at the sun passing far beyond the midday mark. Her eyes felt as if they'd been ground with coarse salt. Each blink rubbed the grains in even deeper. Sunburned. What she'd give for a pair of shades.

Derek nudged her. "Did you see that?"

"What?"

"Something moved in the forest on the other side of that stream." He lowered his paddle and pointed across the water at the distant forest, thick in some places, sparse in others. "Something big."

She followed his gaze beyond a silty stream; the sound of water played everywhere. "Maybe it was a bear."

"No way. It didn't move like a bear. Has anyone around here ever mentioned Bigfoot?"

"Don't be stupid."

"I'm not. I know what a bear looks like. I've been to the San Diego Zoo. It wasn't a bear, Cody. That thing I saw stood up straight and walked like a person."

"Out here?" A wave of gooseflesh rose on her already chilled skin. Déjà vu. She'd experienced the same sensation at the waterfall the day before. For an instant she'd wondered if something had scared the bear away.

"It was probably a shadow." Cody searched for an answer that made sense. "If the angle of the sun was just right, a bear might look like a person. Or maybe it was a tree."

"Right." Derek didn't sound convinced. "A tree that walks."

She turned on her sleeping bag and water oozed

from the goose-down lining. He had her on that one. For the first time since they'd battled the assaulting waves a few hours earlier, she really looked at her cousin. His hair was a matted mess, stuck to the bloody mosquito bites across his forehead. Watery blisters covered the freckles on his nose, and sea salt had dried on his cheeks in crusty white splotches.

"You know what?" she asked. "You look like a character in an Indiana Jones movie."

"Yeah?" Derek was shaking. Hunger. Fatigue. Low body temperature. "You look like something in a disaster movie—the disaster."

Cody laughed, then realized her lips were as swollen as her sunburned hands. She pressed her T-shirt against her mouth so that her lips wouldn't split open. The skin on her face felt tight too, as if she'd outgrown it. She hated being so fair, knowing she'd peel in a few days. More freckles.

She tried wiggling her toes. The intense burning in her feet had lessened to a dull ache. The water that had seeped into her boots earlier had now mixed with body heat and created a layer of insulation. "How are your feet?" she asked.

"What feet?"

She took one last look at the iceberg as the kayak slipped around a bend. They left the narrow passage with its steep-sided walls and entered a broad stretch with enticing slopes. The iceberg boomed and cracked and split into a dozen smaller bergs as if in farewell.

"*Bergy bits*," she said. "That's what they call small icebergs. That and *growler ice*."

Not far ahead, a crop of granite boulders crowded together on a long stretch of bank above the waterline. The rocks appeared to have stumbled off the mountain in a landslide, clearing a bus-sized spot in the otherwise dense forest along the way. The clearing looked wide enough for a campfire. There might be room to pitch the tent if they had to.

"Home sweet home," she said.

Cody held the bowline and balanced on the mossy rocks; in the wet climate any bare rock was quickly colonized by mosses and small plants. Shivering, she passed the gear to Derek, who tossed everything into the clearing.

Neither one of them complained about hunger or aching muscles as they worked mechanically in their heavy, wet clothes.

After tying the kayak with enough rope to secure a battleship, they gathered bits of dry grass and piled it in the clearing. A stroke of luck had placed the matches in a plastic bag *and* in the day packs.

She blew on the stream of smoke rising from the dry grass. "As soon as we get this going we'll look for something to eat."

Warmth first, food second. Anywhere else it might be the other way around. But not this far north in Southeast Alaska, in late summer.

Derek worked at breaking the outer limbs off a downed tree, pulling out the drier ones underneath. Leaves and parasitic moss had long since died and fallen off.

She kept fueling the small blaze with twigs. "Need help?"

He shook his head and grunted, dragging a leafless branch over the rocky ground to the fire. "We can use the push-and-burn method."

Working to unload the kayak had warmed Cody's core temperature. Her toes and fingers had finally thawed out. "We have to dry off." She shrugged off her wet T-shirt and shorts, leaving on her sports bra and dance tights.

Derek stripped to paisley surfer shorts, and Cody laughed at how silly he looked, here in the Alaska wilderness in surfer jams. She draped their clothes over the fallen trees. Derek added the tent and the ground cover and squeezed excess water from the sleeping bags before hanging them on the makeshift clothesline.

The sky above Yakutat was still swollen and bruised, with sudden flashes of jagged light. An electrical storm raged on. No light planes would land in Yakutat as long as it was storming, and no planes would leave Juneau.

"Hot roast beef sandwiches and thick chocolate malts less than ten miles away," she said.

"Do they deliver?" he joked.

"I wish."

Cody pulled a squatty branch up to the fire, sat down, and soaked in the warmth. She hoped it wouldn't take long for her clothes to dry. Then she'd look for something to eat. "The storm is probably dumping new snow on Hubbard." Simple math told her that a glacier accumulating more snow and ice than it lost from melting and calving would keep advancing.

Derek joined her by the fire. "Adding more water to the fjord."

She shivered. "Right."

"If we can't paddle back to Yakutat, does that mean we're going all the way to Hubbard?"

His words danced lightly over the fire, just missing the flames. No, they couldn't go back to Yakutat. They'd already tried that. The current wouldn't let them. Continue forward? If Hubbard was blocking the bay, there wasn't any way out. *Stuck.* High on a rocky bluff without food or shelter, and in the face of an oncoming storm.

Derek shoved another branch in the fire. Something dead, deep inside the wood, made it crackle and spit sparks. "It wasn't a tree," he said, scooting closer to the flame.

For a moment Cody thought he was talking about the firewood. Then she knew: the shadow. She rocked slowly with the gentle afternoon breeze. She hadn't stopped thinking about it either. *Him.* All at once she was thinking of "it" as "him."

A poacher after illegal bearskins or otter hides? The outfitters talked about men who lived in the wilderness. Most of them were social dropouts or hiding from something. The shadow could be a poacher, or worse. No one else would be out here so late in the summer.

Someone was up to no good.

8

Cody slipped back into her T-shirt and shorts, then slapped her socks against a rock. Shavings of dried mud fell to the dirt. She picked off the smaller pieces of mud before putting her socks back on. The bear horn took its place on her waistband.

Derek wore "socks" ripped from the sleeves of an extra T-shirt, which looked more like the booties worn by sled dogs. An oversized sweatshirt hung on him like a skirt. His wet jeans still sagged by the fire.

They worked feverishly to pitch the tent, now that it was dry. They secured it against the storm rumbling down the fjord by dragging it against the "wall" of fallen trees. That way it had some protection from wind. Derek pulled the fly extra tight to make sure it didn't touch the tent itself. Anywhere the two materials touched would leak when the rain hit.

Their only pot had been filled with fresh water from a nearby stream. Cody didn't know how long water needed to boil before it was rid of microscopic parasites. Maybe a rolling boil was enough. Then the pot could cool and double as a drinking cup.

At least water will fill our bellies until we find some-thing to eat, she thought.

Derek dumped an armful of twigs inside the tent so that they'd have dry starter wood when it began raining, then took off again, disappearing in the tangles of underbrush.

Adrenaline, Cody thought. *If he stops moving he'll probably collapse.*

Cody made her way down the slippery boulders near the kayak and scanned the brush for berry vines. The water level had risen another foot: a good twenty feet below their camp. A gull squawked and dive-bombed her.

It must have a nest around here, she thought. *A nest with eggs.*

Eggs. Her mouth watered. Scrambled, poached, in an omelet. Cody could almost smell them, sizzling in melted butter with sprinkles of bacon bits. She abandoned her search for huckleberries and salmonberries and focused on crevices between the rocks.

The gull dived at her again and she dropped to her hands and knees. Gulls didn't nest in trees like most birds, she knew. Their nests were on the ground.

Mosquitoes swam up from the rocks, a swarm of bloodsuckers with an appetite as fierce as her own. She batted at them, trying to sweep them away from her face.

There, in a slight indentation in the dirt, lay three splotchy brownish gray eggs. *Food.* She quickly snatched them up and stowed them inside her shirt, all the time fighting the mosquitoes. The eggs were warm and somehow soothing against her skin. She pretended they came from an egg carton in the fridge.

"Derek?" Cody called at the firepit, where smoke kept the mosquitoes away. She slid the eggs one at a time down the side of the pot and used a stick to keep them from hitting the bottom too quickly. "Derek?"

Soft-boiled won't take long. Two, three minutes. *Only eat one*, she told herself. *Save one for Derek. The third for later. Maybe tomorrow's breakfast.*

"One one-hundred," she counted, stoking the fire. "Two one-hundred."

Cody tilted the pan and used the stick to slide out a single egg. *I won't look at it. I'll peel it with my eyes closed. I'll hold my breath while I chew and swallow.*

Then it'll be over.

But after she swallowed she threw up—a deep wrenching that turned her guts inside out. Then dry heaves. Until not a single drop of water was left in her stomach. She heaved until her body shook and her throat burned.

Keeping her eyes tightly shut, she swept dirt and debris with her hands, then stood up and kicked more dirt. When she opened her eyes all she saw was dirt. No feathers or feet. No boiled beak. The idea of eating a baby bird had made her sick. But it *was* just an egg. And she'd wasted it. What she'd give for a toothbrush.

Derek stumbled into the clearing, red-faced and out of breath. He looked ridiculous in his surfer jams. "I found a cabin," he said.

"Cabin?" she repeated. "With walls and a roof?"

He turned and started back. "Come on."

Cody shoved a burning limb farther into the fire, then trailed him through the forest, climbing over dead trees. She tried to keep the limbs from hitting her in the face, her bare arms taking the scratches instead.

The sky had turned mottled gray, like the boulders and the eggshells. *Rain!* she willed to the storm, stumbling over knotted vines rooting on decayed trees. *Just rain! And get it over with!* The clouds looked like a big fat pillow ready to smother them at any moment.

The cabin itself was nearly strangled by the old-growth forest. Three walls of scrap lumber had been pieced together like a wooden quilt. The fourth wall had long since fallen into the cabin, covering the floor with huge splinters. No door. Probably in the fourth wall. One window covered with heavy plastic, now sickly yellow and curled around the edges. The roof was in the best shape, nailed strips of corrugated metal.

"An old fishing cabin." She stepped carefully over the rubble; dust billowed up. It smelled wet and foul, with a hint of dried blood. Something had died in here. "Maybe there's some old gear lying around. Cooking stuff. We could use another pot. To replace the one we lost in my kayak. Or—" She didn't dare say it. *Food.* She swallowed hard. Her throat still burned.

Derek ended the sentence. "Something to eat." He stretched the words out. "What I'd give for a can of peaches."

"We have eggs." Cody knew she had to tell him.

"Back at camp. They're probably hard-boiled by now."

"Eggs?" His dark eyes widened. He looked as if he had the beginning of a beard, but it was just dirt. "Where'd you get them?"

"I found a nest."

Derek must have drooled because he wiped at his chin. "Eggs."

Cody saw a piece of fur sticking out from beneath an old board. She moved closer, seeing a half dozen skins stacked against the wall. A mound of bones was standing in the corner. "No wonder it stinks in here. Darn poachers!"

She followed Derek back to the clearing and sat on a rock, listening to him crack and eat the first egg. She closed her eyes and waited for the sound of retching. It never came.

"Eat the other one," she said, eyes still closed.

"You don't want it?" he asked.

"Huh-uh."

"Maybe we should save it," he said, hesitation in his voice. "You know, in case we're here for a while."

"It'll just spoil."

Cody rubbed her eyes—making them burn, then tear—and listened to him cracking the second egg. It sounded like Patterson cracking his knuckles. Patterson. Dad. Divorce. Tonya. It all seemed so distant, as if it had happened to someone else.

"Rain," she said when the first drop hit her. The fire sputtered and spit streams of black smoke. "Get in the tent."

She hurried to the clothesline and grabbed the sleeping bags; both had dried with the help of the fire. Everything except Derek's worthless jeans was already inside the tent.

Out on the fjord, the water was so calm that it didn't appear to be breathing. Lifeless. Not a single ripple on its watery chest. Thunder cracked overhead like a charge of dynamite. The next sound was sharp and piercing; electricity charged the sky with white light. More thunder. Lightning.

Cody counted the seconds between thunder and lightning and pulled the sleeping bags inside the tent. The dome tent had metal stakes. Not good. They were surrounded by tall trees. It wasn't at all good. Lightning was attracted to metal things, tall things. But there wasn't anyplace else to go. The cabin would offer little protection against biting rain.

Trapped between a rock and a hard place. That was what the outfitters would say.

Cody crawled inside her bag. "It's five miles away," she said, listening intently. "That's not very far for a storm, maybe only minutes."

Suddenly the tent lit up as though it were powered by a hundred stadium lights. The orange dome glowed a blinding, translucent white. Just as quickly it turned midnight black. Thunder roared like artillery fire down the fjord.

Derek scrambled inside his bag as if it could save him. "Is it coming this way?"

Cody stared, eyes wide, listening. "Yeah."

When she was a kid she'd scamper into Patterson's

room during an electrical storm. She'd snuggle under his comforter and cling to the wall next to his bed. Patterson would rub her back. "Don't worry, Cody," he'd whisper. "It's going to be okay."

The next lightning bolt struck farther away. Thunder rumbled somewhere in the distance.

Derek counted the seconds between the flashes of lightning and rolls of thunder. "It's going away, huh?"

"I think so."

"Are you scared?" he asked.

No sense lying. "Yeah."

"I'm not." He said it simply.

Cody stared at him. He looked different in a way she couldn't pinpoint. Older, maybe—on the inside, where it didn't show. "How come?"

He hesitated slightly. "Promise you won't laugh."

She nodded. "Promise."

Derek rubbed at his forehead, trying to scratch around the mosquito bites. The blood had dried to the color of clay soil, cracked and reddish brown. "I want to write down what's happened since we left Yakutat."

Cody didn't say anything so that he'd go on.

"Josh has the brains in the family," he said. "Marc's the jock and Kevin is the troublemaker. I'm going to be a writer."

Cody thought about Derek's brothers and how different they were from each other. She let the idea of Derek being a writer sink in for a minute. It seemed to fit. "Author Derek Jenson. Sure, why not?"

"No, I don't want to be an author. They make up

stuff. I want to write about things that really happen. Like a journalist."

Derek settled in on his back—long and flat like an exclamation point at the end of his sentence.

Cody breathed deeply, letting the quiet sink in. She felt every muscle and tendon in her body. Muscles she hadn't even known she had were throbbing.

She closed her eyes, listening for the distant thunder. But she didn't hear it. So she focused on the silence. Back in California she'd thought of quiet as the lack of sounds: no cars, no neighbors' TVs, no barking dogs. Silence in Alaska was so complete that it grew into a sound itself.

"It's only eight o'clock," Derek said.

For an instant she wondered if he meant eight in the morning or eight at night. She was so tired, disoriented. Either way she would have already eaten, breakfast or dinner.

Eight at night in the tavern, and her mom would be brushing butter on fish fillets, grilling them for the visiting fishermen. Pan-fried potatoes. Tossed green salad. Homemade rolls. But, no, her mom was in Juneau, picking up supplies.

Food. The outfitters always packed first-class meals for their clients, rich people from the Lower Forty-eight who wanted a wilderness experience without eating it. Cody rolled onto her stomach to muffle its growls and waited for sleep to sneak up on her.

Sometime deep in the lost hours of night a chilling scream shattered the silence. It sounded like an animal crying out. Cody remembered a jackrabbit that had been hit by a car in the desert near Bishop, California. That was back in the days when her family had spent vacations together. The rabbit had screamed in agony until it died.

This animal—whatever it was—was suffering terribly.

It sounded as if it was right outside the tent. *A fresh kill*, she thought. *And something is eating it alive.* The cries of torment went on and on. *Just kill it!* she willed. *Stop the suffering!*

She bolted upright in her sleeping bag. Another scream. More piercing than the others.

The whole world was screaming.

It took a few seconds before she understood that the screams, this time, were coming from her. She pressed her palms into her eyes. Her eyes were on fire. Burning as if someone were stabbing them with red-hot pokers.

Derek was shaking her. "Wake up!"

Cody wasn't asleep. This wasn't a dream. She screamed again in terror and pain. The burning was intense. Unbearable. She opened her eyes. White. Everything was white. Impossible. It was still night.

In utter panic she felt for her flashlight and flipped it on. She still couldn't see anything. "Blind," she screamed. "I'm blind!"

Cody thrashed wildly in her sleeping bag, her eyes two blazing furnaces. *Burning, burning.* She bit her lip and tasted blood. "My eyes," she cried, the salt making them sting even more. "I can't see."

All the hours kayaking on the water and no sunglasses. The intense glare off the glacier. Water, ice, and sun, a conspiracy against her. Burned. Her eyes were seriously sunburned. She shook uncontrollably as the shock of it sank in.

I'm blind!

Cody didn't know why Derek had left the tent; she couldn't know that he'd figured out why she was shaking her head violently, slapping at her eyes. He returned with a cold, damp cloth and placed it gently over her face. "Is that better?"

Cody half nodded and pressed the cloth against her eyes. She trembled as Derek stuffed his extra clothes on one side of her. He shoved his sleeping bag up against her on the other side and crawled in for added warmth. Slowly she relaxed a little. She gave way to semiconsciousness, and finally to restless sleep.

• • •

Hours must have ticked off while she floated in and out of consciousness, barely aware of the washcloth being removed, resoaked to make it cold again, then replaced. Or of her fever. She kicked in her sleeping bag, desperate to escape the heat.

Cody opened her eyes a few times to lightness or darkness. Shadows without shapes. "I can't see!" she cried out.

She thought it was Patterson who answered her. "It's okay. Everything's going to be okay."

"Patterson?" Then his voice turned deep like her father's. "Daddy?"

She dropped off again.

The thin line between reality and dreams disappeared; they became welded together by the fever. And thoughts of food: Sometimes she dreamed of eating, even chewing meat of some kind. She gobbled it up, swallowing some of it whole.

Someone wiped her chin.

And Derek's voice filtering through. "Don't die on me, Cody. You can't die."

It seemed as if she laughed. No one died of sunburn. In the desert, maybe. Not in Alaska.

Shock—now, that could be a killer. And pain sometimes killed.

Dreams pelted her from all sides.

Her father boxing up his *World's Greatest Dad* mug, a Father's Day gift. Even in her dream she wanted to throw it, smash it until the ceramic was nothing but powder.

• • •

The night and the following day slipped away, broken by nightmares and pain. She wanted to rip her eyes from their sockets. Drop them into a bucket of ice water.

If she dared open her swollen lids she saw only white. She'd always thought people who couldn't see lived in a world of darkness!

Derek dipped the cloth in water and bathed her eyes. Another cloth. This one on her forehead. Mopping sweat. Was he reading to her? Impossible. Somehow she figured it out: He was writing in his head and reciting aloud everything that had happened since they'd left Yakutat.

Finally the fever broke and she awakened to the sound of rain splattering the tent. She tried opening her eyes, slowly. Her lids were still puffy, but the intense burning had died to a dull sting.

She turned toward the soft snoring. Even in the early-morning light Derek had a shape, although she couldn't pick out his features.

I can see! she exclaimed to herself.

Then she whispered to the sun gods, "Thank you."

A thank-you for letting her off the hook. They could have kept her sight forever.

She felt around for the damp cloth and pressed it against her eyelids. Her face felt as tight as if it were ready to split open like a barbecued sausage.

How long was I out? she wondered. It couldn't have been too long because she wasn't hungry. She should have been ravenous, near starvation. Except for the egg she'd thrown up, she didn't think she'd eaten since their macaroni and cheese casserole—whenever that was.

"You're back," Derek said from his bag. "Are you okay?"

"Better, much better." She kept her eyes closed, bathing them with the cloth. "It must have been that glare off the water and ice. Without shades. Thank God for No Fear. It could have been so much worse if I didn't have a cap."

"You could have worn my shades," he said, handing her a pot of water.

"Then I'd be taking care of you." Cody drank slowly, rinsing away the rotten taste in her mouth. "You fed me, huh?"

"Yeah. For two days."

"I was out of it for two days?" Suddenly she had to pee. She got up and went outside. When she returned she said, "Did I eat something?"

"Some kind of jerky," he said. "Salmon, I think. I ripped it into small pieces and soaked it in water to soften it up. That and crushed pine nuts."

Derek handed her a strip of jerky, watching her tear off a tough bite. After swallowing she felt bloated, as if she'd just eaten a Thanksgiving dinner. Had her stomach shrunk? Then a more important question came to mind.

Salmon jerky in the tent? She felt for the bear horn, relaxing when she located the handle next to her boots. For a moment she tried to wonder where the food had come from. The cabin, maybe?

Then she lay back down, exhausted, and slept.

The next time she woke up it was night. Moonlight filtered ever so faintly through the tent. It was still raining. Now she needed to *see* the rain. She wanted to *taste* it and dance around in it, rejoicing, *I can see!*

Cody crawled across the floor and unzipped the tent. She stuck her hand out, disappointed not to feel raindrops. Below their camp, granite boulders glistened under a cloudless moonlit sky. Although everything was a blur, she could still make out edges. She waited while her eyes focused on the fjord; a mass of icebergs clogged the inlet.

The sound she had thought to be pelting rain was air being released from melting ice; air that could have been trapped inside a glacier for thousands of years. It sounded like a bowl of rice cereal. *Snap. Crackle. Pop.*

"Wow," she whispered.

Derek scooted next to her and gave her a pouch of pine nuts. She fingered the deerskin. The leather wasn't scarred or rotten as she'd expect from something found in the old cabin. The drawstring was coarse braided hair.

She might have been weakened by fever, but her mind was working. "How come we didn't see this and the jerky before?"

Derek didn't answer. He was under the spell of the parading icebergs.

She followed his gaze. Even in the moonlight

some of the bergs sparkled. And they were so unbelievably blue. They had probably come off the glacier
Cody and Derek had watched calving days before.
The bergs were so tightly packed it looked as if someone could ice-walk to the other side of the fjord.

The air seemed surprisingly mild for a clear night
this late in summer. Thirty-five or forty degrees. Or
maybe she'd just gotten used to the cold.

She wondered if it was clear in Yakutat too.

Had their mothers returned to the empty cabin
and found her note on the milk carton? She checked
her watch, her eyes slow to focus on the numbers:
3:00. She pictured a group of volunteers in the tavern
getting last-minute instructions for the rescue opera-
tion. She'd seen lots of search-and-rescue teams on
the news out of Juneau. Hikers, mountain climbers,
sometimes bush planes. Most of those missing were
found in a few days.

Three A.M. At first light they'd be on their way.
Bush planes with pontoons for a water landing,
packed with survival kits. And food.

"He left it," Derek finally said.

"Who? Left what?"

"You know, Bigfoot. But he's really just this big
guy."

She looked at him, still puzzled.

"He left the food, Cody, and I saw him." His next
words sliced through the air. "I even talked to him."

Suddenly she knew who he meant. The shadow.
It. Him. The up-to-no-good man. "You talked to him?
What did he say?"

10

Cody crawled back inside the tent, snatched the damp cloth, and pressed it against her swollen eyes. She must have stared too long at the parade of icebergs. Even without any glare, she could feel the strain. Daylight would be utter torture.

He must be making it up. "You want to be a writer. And this is a story, right?"

Derek rezipped the tent flap. "I don't think he wanted me to see him. I just did, at the cabin."

She pressed the cloth harder against her eyes; the pressure caused a play of colors behind her lids. She remembered the stack of skins under the boards. The pile of bones. "Were those his skins we found?"

The outfitters had talked a lot about poachers, about men who killed animals for their hides and sold them to other countries. Animals hunted without permits, slaughtered out of season. Even animals on the endangered lists. The thought of poachers made her sick.

"Maybe he followed us," she said, considering another possibility.

"I think he was already here. He just saw us, that's all. Knew we were in trouble, knew we needed help."

The same person could have scared off the bear at the waterfall. Maybe the bear had ruined his plans of sneaking up on her. Cody didn't want to think about that.

That had been days and miles behind them. There weren't any roads or trails out here. Except for the maze of trampled brush made by bears. Unless someone else had been on the water. Surely she would have seen a kayak or canoe. Then she remembered Derek spotting a shadow on the far side of the fjord. Maybe the shadow was on this side now.

All at once it was as if the pages of "Hansel and Gretel" were unfolding. Two kids lost in the woods, following bread crumbs to the wicked witch's house. "He's a poacher, Derek. I'd bet anything."

"You don't know that for sure."

Cody dropped the cloth, waiting for her eyes to focus. She could see that some of the scabs from Derek's mosquito bites had been picked off. There were small white spots on his forehead, a stark contrast to the dark circles under his eyes. The blisters on his nose had dried. Now half peeling, the skin underneath was raw and pink.

"Why else would he be out here this late in summer?" she asked.

Derek shrugged.

She shivered, knowing he could be lurking outside the tent at this very moment. "What did he look like?"

Derek hesitated, then described him. The stranger was too much like a character in a late-night movie.

The kind where a scientist travels back in time and discovers a lost civilization. Crude deerskin pants and a poncho-type shirt, homemade boots, scruffy fur cap and gloves.

"It doesn't matter what he looks like." Derek finished, and glanced toward the cabin. "He's trying to help us."

"Said the spider to the fly," Cody said.

"You're just paranoid," he said. "Because of that kidnapping."

Cody sighed, remembering Ginny Martin, the curly-haired little girl who had been snatched from her bed in the middle of the night. The Martins lived only a few miles from Cody's house. Even after a year, the family didn't know what had happened to her. "And you're too trusting of strangers."

Derek quit trying to convince her that the man wasn't a threat. He changed the subject by shining his flashlight on his new project. Part of a torn T-shirt was stretched tightly over a board and secured with old nails. He'd used charred firewood to sketch in the fjord, from Yakutat to Hubbard Glacier at Disenchantment Bay. "I made this map while you were sick."

She saw an X at their first camp. "You were reciting what's happened to us out here."

"Yeah, the map goes with my story."

"I bet one of the papers in Alaska would publish it."

"You really think so?"

"Maybe even the *Californian*." That was the big paper in Bakersfield.

Cody knotted her hair into a fist, which fell lopsided over one ear. Dried salt water mixed with sweat and dirt had made her hair coarse and stiff.

Outside, the sky had started to lighten up. *At least the storm's over*, she told herself. *Mom's found the note by now and a rescue party will be on its way at first light. All we have to do is build a fire and stay put until a pilot spots the smoke.*

Cody fell into the warm folds of her sleeping bag. "You still haven't told me what the poacher said."

"He didn't talk. I did. I thanked him for the food."

"Are you nuts?" She couldn't believe Derek wasn't more suspicious of a stranger in the wilderness. Especially someone dressed in skins. "No wonder your mom worries so much about you."

"Maybe if you talked to him you wouldn't be so scared."

"I'm not scared," she said quickly. "I'll start socializing with poachers when the fjord freezes over."

Derek sighed, settling deeper into his bag.

Cody wouldn't talk about it anymore. In a little while they'd build a roaring fire. Under a clear sky, smoke would be visible for miles. "Yakutat." She rolled it around on her tongue. Hot shower, hot meal. She'd sell her soul for the shower alone. No, a toothbrush. Brushing her teeth would even beat a shower.

"Let's not wait on the fire," she said. "Let's get it going now."

• • •

Cody huddled with her back to the fire pit, shielding her eyes from the heat and light. She'd pulled her knotted hair through the back of No Fear; the brim shaded her eyes. Maybe she'd rub mud high on her cheekbones. That was what Patterson did when he played football to absorb the beams off stadium lights.

She wished she had lotion to rub on her face. It was so hard and dry it felt ready to crack. She considered searching for edible roots, something that wasn't toxic. She could boil and mash them, then spread them on her face. But by the time she went to all that trouble the rescuers would be there.

Now that the skies over Yakutat were rid of thunderstorms, their rescue was inevitable, probably within an hour, certainly before lunchtime, a thought that took the edge off images of a poacher dressed in dead animals.

At sunrise the sky spread soft-colored pastels; then a heavy gray mist muddied the palette. Even in a fire pit clogged with burning logs the smoke evaporated into the clouds.

If you don't like the weather, wait five minutes, she reminded herself.

The water had risen another five or six feet since she'd been out of it. Luckily the terrain was steeper here than at their first campsite, and the tent was still high above the waterline. No sea life swam by, no otters, no porpoises. And few birds. Where were all the deer? There were more deer in Southeast Alaska than people, she knew. She hadn't seen one since they'd left Yakutat.

Now that she was sure help was on the way she'd stopped worrying so much about the tide. She kept glancing at the fjord, noting that the icebergs had vanished. They must be melting or drifting around another bend. She strained to see that the kayak was safely tethered.

"Where are the planes and helicopters?" she asked an hour later.

Sitting sideways, she stoked the coals with a stick. Fiery sparks sputtered around her boots, quickly snuffed out by the soupy mist. "Wouldn't choppers fly in from Juneau to search for a couple of kids lost in the fjord? And there are lots of bush planes in Yakutat."

She realized she was talking to herself. The sound of leaves crunching in the trees made her jump. "Derek?"

Instinct pushed her fingers to one of the logs, guiding them around the rough bark. *If it's a bear, I hope it's a black bear. I'd rather face a black bear than a grizzly any day. If it's the poacher, I might still need a weapon.*

Slowly rising to her feet, she turned, letting her eyes focus on the vine-tangled woods, drab brown and muted green like military camouflage.

"Derek?"

Be quiet! Hold the log behind your back . . . The instructions were coming from some other self, her survival self. Then, at the last second . . .

Staring this long was painful, but she didn't dare blink.

She stood still, hands gripping the log, and waited.

Derek moved into the clearing. "What're you doing?"

Cody tossed the log in the fire. *"Me?"* She noticed for the first time that he was back in his jeans, the cuffs tucked inside his rubber boots; three days and a fire must have been long enough to dry them. "You scared me to death. I didn't know you'd left."

Derek rubbed his hands briskly over the fire. "I thought you were sleeping, so I went to the cabin."

"What for?"

He pulled a T-shirt scrap from under his sweatshirt. "I found some berries."

She recognized the pink fruit, smooth and succulent. Salmonberries. "He left them, didn't he?"

Derek shrugged.

"Did you see him?"

She looked nervously toward Yakutat. *Where is the search party?* she cried to herself. Then she turned to Derek and said aloud, "What does he want from us?"

He set the bundle in the dirt, the T-shirt becoming a platter. *"I* found the berries."

Cody thought he was lying but didn't argue about it. She snatched a handful of berries and ate them quietly. She needed to build up her strength. The juice had an odd taste, not as sweet as usual.

They aren't ripe, she thought, eating them anyway.

Derek pulled a strip of brittle plastic from his hip pocket. "Maybe we can make you some shades."

Cody recognized the plastic from the cabin's crude window. She turned it over in her hand. Maybe if she soaked off the years of grime, tucked it under No Fear, notched out a slot for her nose . . . She held it up to her eyes and looked at the flames; the light was definitely softened. But her vision was close to zero.

"Maybe if I can scrape off some of the yellow," she said, hoping she'd never need them.

She was suddenly ravenously thirsty, as if her sunburn had spent the last three days sucking moisture from every pore. She lifted the cooled pot and drank what was left, guzzling each drop. Then she reached for the second pot, swirling it to cool the water.

Derek polished off his half of the berries and dug into the roots. Boiled roots? He couldn't have found roots and boiled them. So the man had either given him the food or left it in the cabin.

"Maybe we'll make sunglasses the way the Eskimos did," Derek said. "I read about it at the lodge. They carved them out of wood, with slits in the front, so you can see out but light can't get in. And we need a fishing pole. We could bend a nail for a hook."

She had to tell him about the note and that she'd sort of cheated on the bet. She hadn't *told* anyone where they had gone, but . . .

Derek took the empty pots and turned in the direction of the stream. "I'll get more water." He paused to look at a white-gray sky tightly knitted with weeping mist. "Then let's start on a fishing pole. The fjord must be full of fish."

She couldn't let him go to the stream yet. "I have good news and bad news," she said.

Derek turned, straddling the downed tree trunk, a pot in each hand.

"The good news is my mom knows we took the kayaks, that we were camping in the fjord. The bad news is I cheated on our bet. I left a note."

He looked as if he'd just choked on a bunch of berries.

"So we don't need a fishing pole." It sounded like an apology, but the note was going to save their lives.

"I don't have any good news," he said. "Just bad news."

Cody waited.

"I found the note . . . and tore it up."

11

The stage was set for a fight, a knock-down, drag-out brawl.

Cody only swore once and tagged it with his name. It came out sounding like one word, *dammitderek.* "Why?"

He shrugged, looking guilty and sorry. "I thought someone might find the note before we got to camp out. People are always going into your cabin." Then he disappeared with pots in hand, heading for the stream.

The mist turned to light rain, adding grayness to the already sullen sky. Shadows on the distant mountains deepened in the valleys. Up close the forest looked like what it was, a dense growth of trees and underbrush choking hundreds of thousands of acres. Farther away it was dead green, the color of lettuce forgotten in the vegetable bin.

Cody slipped into her yellow slicker.

No one knows we're here, she thought.

Except the poacher.

Derek would continue to the stream for water; then he'd probably head to the cabin for nails: fish-hooks. She should have gone with him, but she'd been so ticked off about the note.

The fire kicked up when the drizzle lightened to an annoying mist. Fire and smoke were still allies.

Would a search party start at the beach, on the ocean side? She and Derek had gone to the beach every day it hadn't rained since he'd come to Yakutat. Their mothers knew the routine: hang out at Cannon Beach, a fifteen-mile-stretch with fifteen- to twenty-foot breakers that attracted surfers from around the world. Check out the fishing action, chat with the locals.

How many days would it take before the canvas bags holding their kayaks were missed? No one used them this late in the season. She had another thought: Her mom might even think they'd been kidnapped.

Now that Cody knew about the stranger, she couldn't stay another night. They needed to pack up and get back in the kayak. No one could sneak up on them on the water.

Cody sank into the brush behind the tent to pee. That was when it hit her that Derek now had two pots—and they didn't *have* a second pot. One had disappeared with her kayak and the rest of the gear. But she'd recognized the second one. It *was* theirs— one of a matching pair purchased at Mustache Pete's General Store in Yakutat.

She'd just zipped her shorts when Derek returned to the clearing. She closed her eyes, waiting for them to stop stinging. Her eyes needed lots of rest; it still took time before objects farther than ten feet away were more than blurs.

She had to ask Derek about the second pot. Maybe it had fallen out of her kayak when it capsized and had washed ashore.

He was leaning into the tent when she moved up on him. "Derek? Where did—"

She stopped.

It wasn't her cousin.

Slowly the man turned . . .

"What do you want?" she shouted.

He didn't answer.

Make yourself big. Don't let him know you're afraid.

It had worked with the bear.

Her eyes were fully focused on the man twenty feet in front of her. She realized he was wearing the crude deerskin clothes Derek had described. But all she saw was his mask. A dark patch tied over his nose and cheeks, butting into a white beard. His eyes were dark and threatening.

The man's beard shook as if he was going to say something. Cody imagined a low, guttural grunt like that of a wild animal. That was what he looked like: an animal.

"*Get out of here!*" she screamed, and stumbled backward, bumping into the woodpile. She was about to scream again when he clutched at his mask, as if he wasn't sure he was wearing it. Just as suddenly he spun around and fled the clearing.

Cody stood stiff and alert. She kept her eyes on the trees and reached down to the woodpile. Her fingers found a board studded with nails. A scrap from the cabin.

If he came back, she'd let him have it, without a second thought.

Her skin crawled under the slicker. She'd never seen anyone, *anything* like him before. He reminded her of the old circus poster in her grandmother's garage. Faded and yellow, it touted Mr. Apeman, supposedly raised from birth by gorillas in a jungle.

The mask . . . the fur gloves . . . it wasn't that cold.

He's hiding something.

Ten minutes ticked off, then twenty. Not so much as a breeze rustled in the trees. Still, he could be watching.

Waiting was the worst part.

She snatched a second board from the pile. *I'm going to look for Derek.*

With two boards in hand she crawled over the fallen trees, tensing at every sound. Her boots crushed dead branches, splashed shallow puddles, sucked soft mud.

The forest had been trampled into a path. Derek must have trudged back and forth many times in the past few days.

The vegetation was a tight weave in some places, and the boards were awkward to carry. Heat from rotting debris seemed inconsistent with the drizzle. The steam bubbled up from the ground, working its way under her slicker and mixing with her nervous sweat. Sweat even dripped from No Fear.

She constantly scanned the trees, expecting the man to jump out.

What was he doing in our tent?
Go check the cabin.

Derek would have stopped to look for nails to make fishhooks with, after filling the pots at the stream. Her eyes still burned but she didn't allow herself more than a blink. And her sunburned face was itching.

The cabin looked different than it had three days before. Most of the old boards had been sorted into piles of scraps and usable wood. Derek's handiwork. He must have thought they'd be stranded for a while. He'd even swept the floor. A crude branch broom leaned against the wall. The stack of skins had disappeared with the pile of bones.

She gripped her boards more tightly and whispered, *"Derek!"*

He wasn't there.

It was still and dark on the path leading to the stream, with barely enough air to breathe. Mosquitoes sprang from the ground and she batted at them with the boards. She shook her head to keep the whining bloodsuckers away.

They had to get back in the kayak. She'd rather face calving glaciers and rolling icebergs than a monster.

They could fish and trail a baited line behind the kayak. Clean it, eat it. *Raw.* Sushi was popular in California.

She'd even sit in the rear seat if she had to, and rest her eyes. Derek would like that.

She still couldn't believe he had torn up the note.

Cody stood at the stream, the boards hanging at her side. *"Derek!"* she whispered again. *"Where are you?"*

Upstream, the outline of two pots developed edges as her eyes slowly focused. One was on its side, the other upside down. The appearance of the second pot hammered at her. Maybe her kayak hadn't broken free on the rising tide after all. Maybe the bowline had been cut.

"Derek!"

No answer.

She caught sight of her frightening reflection in a shallow pool. Her eyes were puffy; her face was scratched, dirty, and streaked with smoke. It looked as if the muddy ground had reached up and slapped her. Her hair was a mass of tangles springing from No Fear.

She dropped the boards in the water, shattering the image.

"Derek!" she called again.

Silence.

She knew the poacher had him.

12

Cody rushed back to the campsite, trying to quiet the screaming in her head. The frightening words were like a hundred schoolyard bullies ganging up on her, until she shouted, *"No!"*

This can't happen to someone in my family.

Derek dropped the pots by the stream to go berry picking. That's it. He'll march back any second with salmonberries stuffed in his sweatshirt.

But Cody couldn't ignore the truth. The man had him. A setup. Baited with decoys: berries and roots. Tricked into trusting a poacher.

Kidnapped.

At the thought of the word *kidnapped* she stumbled down the slick granite boulders below camp. She slipped on loose rock and shale, making her way to the kayak, where she worked frantically on the stubborn knot.

The line had been soaked by dew and drizzle, dried and soaked again, saturated with salt air, probably dozens of times in the last several days. The knot was hard and tight. She ripped one of her fingernails and blood dripped onto the knot. But it refused to give in. If she had an ax she could slice its twisted neck.

The sun briefly broke through the sluggish gray sky. Above her boots and below her slicker blood was seeping through her dance tights. A sticky splotch the size of the knot in the bowline. Most likely a puncture wound, she thought, from a nail in one of the boards. She'd never even felt it.

Pull yourself together! she told herself. Without an ax she couldn't free her kayak. She needed to tend to her wound. And be more careful.

Cody scrambled back up the incline, stopped, and panted. Mud clung to her boots, making them heavy and awkward. She couldn't afford a mistake now. Mistakes were what had put them in this mess in the first place.

Forcing herself to think more clearly, she snatched the torn T-shirt off the clothesline and wrapped it around her leg.

Think! she insisted. Then it came to her.

The poacher and Derek couldn't have gone down the fjord as she had first thought. There weren't any new tracks leading to the water. They must have gone by land. Then she remembered the abandoned pots on the sandy banks of the stream. That was where she'd start her search.

Cody decided to pack up some of her stuff. Crawling partway in the tent, she grabbed her sleeping bag and started rolling it up.

Her hands continued moving across the floor. Derek's clothes and bag were gone. Even his map of the fjord. All gone.

That was what the man had been doing in the

tent. Stealing Derek's stuff. He must have come back when she went to the cabin.

She found another deerskin bundle, twice the size of the first one. Inside were heaps of jerky, seeds, berries, dried roots.

Why did he leave me food?

It's another trick.

"I will not cry."

Then, because she had never thanked Derek for taking care of her and feeding her, she broke down and sobbed.

I'm going to find Derek and get him back.

She packed the wild man's food and the flashlight. The bear horn was already in place. She stuffed everything else in her daypack, including her slicker, and tied her sleeping bag to the outside.

Cody looked around the clearing, taking in the details of the camp. Leaving was scary but she couldn't think about that now. She'd already wasted too much time. The sky was depressing in its grayness, thick and damp. But she was grateful. Sunshine would have been utter torture.

She pushed through mudholes and snagged her clothes on vines, struggling unsteadily with the heavy pack pulling on her back. She glanced at her watch: an automatic reflex; 9:30. At home she'd still be asleep.

At the stream Cody stood over the two pots. They stared at her with hollow black eyes. Beyond the pots she discovered footprints in the damp sand. The wafflelike patterns left from Derek's boots were the same as her own, only three sizes larger.

The poacher's prints, she noted, were flat. No insteps or heels. Just flat fur boots, probably fur from some animal he'd killed. She shivered.

Then she moved to the edge of the stream, untied the T-shirt bandage, and washed her wound as best she could through her tights. Her thigh was sore from the rusty nail. She soaked her bandanna and bathed her eyes.

She walked ahead. Suddenly the footprints stopped. Drizzle had washed away all signs of life. The prints picked up farther into the woods—not prints exactly, just trampled leaves and broken vines.

Every step up the mountain moved her away from both the camp and the kayak, away from Yakutat. But closer to Derek and Wildman. That was how she thought of the man in skins now. Wildman.

Cody steadied her gaze on the stretch of ground in front of her. One boot, then the other, following a trail to uncertainty.

No. She cut her thoughts midstream. *I'm following a path to certainty.*

Certain danger.

13

Early in the afternoon Cody climbed a VW-sized boulder by clinging to heavy vines. Mud had washed over the rock, making it as slippery as owl manure, as the old-timers would say.

The mud itself was a reddish clay, almost an exact match with the blood-stained T-shirt wrapped around her leg. Even her black boots were mud colored.

Cody stopped at a bend in the trail. She closed her eyes a moment to let them rest and listened to her strained breathing. The point overlooked the fjord and she let her eyes slowly take it all in, surprised she'd hiked this far. The water was spread out below her several miles away. The inlet really did resemble a lake from here; the steep rock walls looked like stepping stones.

She wondered why there weren't any environmentalists in the fjord trying to rescue seals, porpoises, and other trapped animals. There should be *National Geographic* reporters and photographers, since Hubbard was named after the first president of the National Geographic Society.

Surrounded by mountains and forest, she caught herself wondering about the altitude, a question one of the outfitters' clients had asked. The obvious answer was sea level.

I am losing it, she told herself, *if I'm trying to remember stuff that basic.*

She shook her head and turned her thoughts to a trail that could've been made by either a bear or a moose. If Wildman lived in the woods, the route could be his. But *trail* was the wrong word. This was little more than a primitive path where underbrush had been stomped down.

She rested a few minutes longer, wishing she could splash cold water on her face. Her bandanna was the same brownish red as everything else. Still, she held the damp cloth against her eyes. Worry weighed her down, making every step a feat worthy of applause.

Clues came in the form of displaced leaves, which would have been slapped onto a boot, carried a few steps, then sloughed off. A puddle that had splashed mud a little too high on a tree. A vine broken at an odd angle. All signs of intruders.

Another boulder filled the path. But this one was no VW. The same slippery marks painted its face, marks made by Derek's and Wildman's boots.

The trail was nearly vertical here, a cliff face of unsettled shale. If the rock had handholds and footholds she couldn't see them. Too much mud. Halfway up the hump in its back, a vine made a lazy S. If she could get hold of it, she was sure she'd be able to pull herself up.

She took a running start and scrambled up the rock face, trying to swipe at the vine to dislodge it.

She'd forgotten about her pack. The extra weight threw her off balance and she fell backward, landing hard. Her leg started bleeding again.

I'm a complete mess.

A failure.

I can't do this.

The mosquitoes found her again. *Bloodsucking demons!*

Then the sun broke through and the mosquitoes disappeared. Even though she had to squint against the light, the warmth felt good against her back. She tugged on the brim of No Fear until it shaded her face.

I won't quit until I'm dead.

As if in response, a bird with a menacing wingspan circled high overhead. She strained for a better look but the sky was too bright for her sore eyes.

They probably had buzzards in Southeast Alaska. The ugly black birds ruled California's highways, thriving on roadkill.

They smell the blood on my leg.

She dredged the torn shirt in mud and rebandaged her wound. The mud felt cool, soaked up some of the sting. Then she set her mind on getting the vine.

In the end it wasn't that hard; a dead branch hooked the vine on the third try. Now that the vine was straight, it reached easily to the ground. She looped it through her pack, left the pack at the base of the rock, and started climbing. One toehold, then another. She kept hold of the vine in case she slipped. Near the top she glanced down at her pack.

Big mistake.

Flushed with heat, she broke out in a sweat. Her fingers felt strange and alien, as if they were gripping handlebars on a bike instead of strangling a vine.

If I cry I'll die.

Her boot slipped. She dangled helplessly, trying to regain her footing. She felt as if she had just run the Los Angeles Marathon in place, all but the last stretch of its twenty-six miles. Only a few more steps until she crossed the finish line.

She pressed her boots into the rock and moved up slowly, not daring to look down again—praying she wouldn't slip and find herself on the ground. It seemed to take forever; near the end she was pulled up by thoughts of Derek.

On top, she collapsed, so weak that she couldn't stand right away. But she'd made it. Then she crawled away from the edge and glanced at her watch. The face was shattered, the hands stopped. She tossed it in the brush and pulled up her pack, the vine still looped through the straps.

On this stretch of trail the undergrowth choked the path to almost nothing. Everything was so unbelievably green. Spruce and hemlock, and all kinds of shrubs she couldn't name.

Earlier she'd eaten some jerky and half the berries. Wildman's food. She munched another boiled root. The roots were as sharp as onions and just as slimy. At least they were moist.

Her mouth tasted metallic, like dirt and nails mixed together. Add a little fish jerky . . . She ran her finger over her teeth. Five days without a toothbrush.

After eating she hiked on, encouraged by a print made by Derek's boots, now a step behind the wide flat prints of Wildman.

Her own boots slipped on her heels; her socks were matted with mud. *Extra insulation*, she thought, *added warmth*.

Cody stopped.

"No." She shook her head.

It wasn't possible.

She knelt down and drew her finger through the damp earth.

A third set of prints trudged down the trail; smaller than Wildman's, but pressed by the same type of homemade boot.

There could only be one answer and she knew it. Wildman had a partner.

14

Until now she'd tried not to think about what she would do after she caught up to Derek and Wildman. She'd counted her steps, her breaths—anything to *not* think about it, hoping she'd come up with a plan and spring into action when the time came.

Adrenaline will kick in. The whisper came on the edge of consciousness. *Instinct will take over.*

Now everything had changed. There was another person. But she still had to find Derek.

Fog moved in on the mountain in front of her, from the ocean end of Russell Fjord, where the Pacific Ocean filled Yakutat Bay. Fog from the sea, but as white as bleached bones in the desert. It moved like water tumbling down the mountain, wiping out vast sections of trees. Seconds later it lifted and framed a rock outcropping, then dropped just as quickly and obliterated the entire scene.

Cody spun around, startled by a sound shattering the mountain silence. The sound was foreign. She listened, clinging tightly to the straps of her pack.

Her gaze scanned the nearby woods. She could see up to ten feet in some directions, depending on light and vegetation. She made herself smaller, squatting down.

The noise grew in intensity.

Cody jumped up and let the sound of rotary blades wash over her: a helicopter. "I'm down here!" she yelled at the chopper, hearing it somewhere above her.

"Here I am!" Her leg began bleeding again. She quickly untied the T-shirt bandage and waved the bloody flag in the air. "Down here!"

First I'll tell them about Derek, then Wildmen. They won't stand a chance now. Their game is finished!

Cody dropped her pack. She thought about climbing a tree and tying the T-shirt on top like an SOS. But even the lower branches were too high, so she just waved the bloody shirt, screaming, "I'm down here!"

The sound grew less intense.

It's looking for a place to land, she told herself. *There has to be a place somewhere!*

The pilot must have seen the fire and the tent. He must have spotted the kayak. The sound of whirling blades faded to a flat hum, like that of distant bees. *Looking for a place to land; looking for a place!*

They know I'm down here. We're down here.

Don't panic!

Finally the sound vanished into the mist.

She laughed like someone on the verge of madness. *Back to Yakutat for reinforcements—that must be it!*

Cody collapsed on the ground and rubbed fresh mud over her wound. The T-shirt again took its place as a bandage. It would have been easy to make an arrow with rocks. An arrow in the clearing near the tent pointing to the stream, leading them to the abandoned pots, eventually to Wildmen's trail.

The neglected fire and empty tent would tell them the camp was deserted.

Cody shrugged into her pack. She saw a feather on the ground in a bed of leaves. Probably a buzzard feather. Picking it up, she recognized it as belonging to an eagle. An eagle?

"I can't even tell the difference between a buzzard and an eagle!" she said aloud.

And then to herself: *I don't belong out here alone.*

Up the mountain, the fog parted again. This time the opening highlighted a section of trail on steep, rugged terrain with few trees. Three beetle-sized dots stuck out against the pale granite: all three moving, hunched over, as if searching the ground for something lost.

"Derek," she muttered.

Then the fog returned and swallowed them up.

At least he wasn't hurt. The rescuers would be coming soon. *Don't worry, help is on the way.*

Hour after hour *Don't worry, Derek* repeated itself in Cody's mind as she walked the trail that no longer climbed up the mountain. She was now walking parallel to the fjord and moving in the direction of Hubbard. In some places the ground was so wet that it was like walking on a soggy sponge.

Still, no sounds.

No chopper or airplane.

It didn't make sense.

Maybe the windswept water was too rough for a seaplane. Maybe the fjord was too narrow. She strained to hear the sound of a boat or plane engine. Then she stopped and looked around for a place to hold up. She knew she'd have to sleep under a roof of branches. Parcel out jerky and berries for dinner, save some for tomorrow. Suddenly the tent back in camp seemed like a five-star hotel.

Four days earlier she'd poked fun at Derek for dividing trail mix. Now she was doing the same thing.

Fog. Maybe that was why no one had come back. Fog was as dangerous as thunderstorms, and grounded just as many flights. Boats and cars piled up in the pea soup.

She tossed her pack under a tree, spread her slicker on the ground. Sitting on her sleeping bag, she untied the bandage to look at her leg. Dried blood mixed with dried mud. She winced, knowing that the pain that had left her eyes had now settled into her thigh.

The next day rescuers would wind their way down the fjord. The next day Derek would be saved and Wildmen would have to face the authorities.

The next day would be marked *The End*.

She'd tell Derek, "You can drive the old pickup when we get back."

Cody pulled down No Fear, trying to cut out the menacing night sounds. She shivered down to her bones. Was it the night air or her own anxiety? She tried sleeping on her side, then on her back, always keeping the pressure off her leg. She wadded up her sweatshirt but it felt more like a rock than a pillow.

This only happened to people on the news. Not to normal people like her and Derek. Then she remembered Ginny Martin.

The strange night sounds reminded her just how alone she was and how little she knew about anything. She looked in the direction of the sunset, a faint glow setting off jagged peaks blacker than night itself, and worried about Derek.

They'll have to take care of him, she tried to reassure herself. *Otherwise he isn't worth anything to them.*

Cody just couldn't unwind, couldn't turn off her brain.

The night went on and on.

Cody moaned in her sleep when something told her that she was surrounded by water, that she wasn't just dreaming about drowning but was actually inhaling salt water and choking. She didn't have any idea where she was or what was happening.

Dial 911.

But her finger punched in a different set of numbers, seven digits plus an area code: three-one-zero. Her finger kept slipping on the last number.

More than once she'd actually dialed all seven digits without fumbling. After an agonizing number of rings a stranger answered, "You're looking for Mr. Lewis? He moved three years ago. And his new number is unlisted."

She'd had the same dream off and on since the divorce. Calling her dad now didn't make sense. Even in a dream she should have been dialing the lodge in Yakutat.

It took several minutes before she fully awakened, drifting in and out of a foggy reality. One second she was in the kayak battling four-foot waves, the next she was staring into the face of a masked madman. Then it was all reality. She was sleeping out in the open in a remote Alaskan wilderness.

Cody rolled over and cried out when her weight pressed her thigh. Her first instinct was to check her watch. Stupid. She knew first light meant it was four A.M. And besides, her watch was broken and she'd thrown it away.

The blue-gray clouds hung in layers stacked across the mountains where the sun would make its first appearance. Even without sore eyes, the sky was so alive behind the weaker clouds that she had to look away. Cody usually liked the hours between first light and sunrise.

Her sleeping bag was damp on the outside. Still, she pulled it over her torn clothes and willed her body to make heat. She imagined the pilots in Yakutat in the tavern, filling mugs with steaming coffee. Her mom would be scrambling eggs and frying sausage, which would be gobbled while planes were being fueled for the rescue flight.

Eggs and sausage. Strange that the idea of food didn't make her hungry. No gnawing pangs or grumbles. Her stomach remained a dead void taking up space in her body.

The pilot must have seen their camp yesterday. *Soon*, she thought.

She snuggled deeper into her bag, barely aware of her aching muscles, bruises, and scrapes, focusing on wiggling her half-numb toes.

Cody wondered if Derek and Wildmen were

working their way down the trail. Holding the sleeping bag around her shoulders, she sat up and cringed at the pain in her leg. She couldn't believe she'd slept through the night.

The air held its usual dampness, heavy with its own wet weight. The bottom of her bag had slipped off her rain slicker; in places it was as wet and muddy as the rest of the landscape. Everything around her was shiny with dew.

The clouds were dissolving over the horizon. She blinked at the brightening sky and pulled the brim of her cap down. Her eyes only burned a little today. They certainly weren't hurting as badly as the heat in her leg.

She peeled back her bag, startled by the sight of her clothes. Ripped, muddy, spotted with dried blood. Her hands appeared to have battled barbed wire and lost. Her nails were jagged and torn.

She studied the bandage, still in place and wrapped loosely around her thigh. It untied easily enough but refused to loosen from her skin. Maybe a scab was forming. She inspected the skin around the bandage. It wasn't pretty but the swelling had started to go down.

Cody retied the T-shirt, careful not to yank on it. She forced herself to choke down a strip of jerky, then licked the last of the squashed berries off the deerskin cloth that had held them. The berries were sickeningly sweet now, too ripe. Scooting out of her sleeping bag, she stood up and laughed as her shorts nearly fell off. She couldn't believe she'd lost that much weight.

She used the filthy bandanna as a belt, then hooked on the bear horn.

At least there aren't any mosquitoes, she thought, pulling the slicker over her sweatshirt for added warmth. She forced her feet into her dirty socks, then slipped into her boots and found a couple of walking sticks.

Moving down the trail, she concentrated on the sky, which would soon be filled with planes and helicopters. *Soon, Derek.* She no longer dreamed of a hot bubble bath or brushing her teeth. None of that mattered now.

For the first time since she'd left camp the day before, she started making plans. The bear horn. It could be used as a diversion, drawing Wildmen away from Derek. First she'd have to figure out how to set it off without touching it. If only she had some fishing line; she could tie it around the trigger, string the line over the ground.

Cody noticed her steps slowing; she was relying heavily on the walking sticks. Sometimes she'd catch a whiff of her own breath. It was just as disgusting as she'd always imagined a bear's breath would be. *Bears.* She fingered the horn. She wondered why they weren't bothering her.

Lost in thought, she hardly noticed the miles falling behind her. She searched the sky for rescuers. Maybe she hadn't really seen a helicopter the day before. People stumbling around in the desert saw all kinds of things that weren't real. Maybe that happened to people in the wilderness.

There had been signs of life on the trail earlier. But she couldn't tell how long ago the prints had been made. Some of them were filled with heavy dew; others were little more than muddy smears.

Were Derek and Wildmen still ahead of her? Or had they circled back?

The answer seemed as clear as dew dripping off leaves. *Steal the tent and kayak. Destroy all signs of life. Make it harder on the rescuers.* She leaned against a tree, resting a minute. *But if Wildmen wanted to get rid of our gear, they could have done it before now.*

Suddenly her questions and answers seemed as muddied as a muskeg bog. She wasn't sure of anything.

Back on the trail, a thinning stand of trees in the distance was being invaded by ground fog. Her heart sank. Fog could halt rescue efforts. *Please don't roll in. Not now.*

As she moved down the trail, closing in on the white mist, she realized it wasn't fog at all. *Smoke*— from a campfire! It rose from the ground, twisting and licking the air above the trees. Wildmen.

More alert than she had been in days, she sloughed off her pack and shoved it under a tree. *Derek?* The smoke wasn't more than two hundred yards away. Still, she wasn't about to rush into Wildmen's camp. She had to move up on them slowly, quietly.

Like a predator stalking its prey, she crept through the trees toward the fire.

16

Cody picked her way over the soggy ground toward the smoke. She kept herself small, aiming from tree to tree. The cold had a sharper bite this morning. Summer was finally waving the flag, surrendering to autumn.

Then voices hit her. They absorbed her, played against her skin. She held her breath.

Voices. Low and dull. She couldn't understand the words. She strained to hear Derek.

Closer, I've got to get closer.

She let herself breathe slowly through her mouth and inched her way through ferns and rusty manzanita.

The talking stopped abruptly.

Cody stood still.

She listened.

A glacial wind whipped around the trees. The cold sapped her strength. The body used a ton of energy to keep warm, burned a ton of fat to make heat. She hadn't had much fat to begin with. Suddenly she understood why people in subzero climates ate whole cubes of butter.

Fire and smoke.

She crept closer.

Everything was suspended, as if the earth had stopped spinning.

Then she saw it, about seventy-five feet away. An opening in the trees much like the clearing that had held their tent so many miles back.

Derek was settled on a boulder near the fire pit, holding a stick over the blaze. *Breakfast.* The idea was slow to sink in. It seemed so ordinary. *He's cooking breakfast!*

Just seeing him, knowing he was okay, gave her more strength than any amount of food, sleep, or warmth. She let out her breath, unsure what to do next.

No one else was in the clearing; at least she couldn't see anyone. She wanted to shout, but she didn't dare. Not yet. She had to watch for a while. Watch *them.* Where were Wildmen?

Derek was wearing a crude animal-skin poncho. His hands weren't tied, but she couldn't see his ankles. The fire pit blocked her view. She wondered who had been talking. Where were they now?

She studied the shack on the far side of the clearing. Four sides with a wooden roof. A door of stripped limbs tied with rawhide. The shack had a few scraps from the old cabin. She recognized the same rotten, worm-eaten wood.

It looks like it's been here for years, she thought.

The smell of meat reached out to her. Fat dripped in the fire, spitting and sizzling. The void in her stomach begged for something fresh to eat. Derek pulled a piece of charred fat off the meat—chewed bite after bite, licked grease off his fingers, wiped grease off his chin.

Cody swallowed hard.

She heard the door creak before it opened. Derek turned his head toward the person backing out of the hut. One of the Wildmen. She touched the bear horn, an automatic reflex. If nothing else she could throw it at him.

Wildman turned, set a pot on the fire.

Where was the fur mask? The gloves? The wild mangy hair? This guy was dressed in the same skin pants and homemade boots. But no, it wasn't possible.

Cody closed her eyes, not believing the picture: *Her* hair was gathered in a neat braid.

It didn't make any sense. It made perfect sense.

The second pair of prints, like Wildman's only smaller—a woman's boots. The woman was short but sturdy looking, her face smooth and round. Seashells were stitched in double rows along a wool poncho where the dark blue came together with the red material. Larger shells and bones dangled like bells from the top of her mukluks. Sealskin, it looked like.

Cody recognized her as Tlingit, a member of the largest native population in Southeast Alaska. Half of Yakutat had Tlingit ancestry.

Derek didn't seem bothered by her presence. *Maybe it's some kind of act. He's just playing it cool until he can get away.*

The woman's mukluks rattled when she walked

back to the shack. Cody leaned closer, trying to see inside when the door opened. But it was too dark.

Derek! She willed him to look at her. *Derek!*

He poked his stick through another slab of raw meat without even a glance in her direction.

Cody decided to sneak back to her pack, settle in, and wait. Maybe there was a little jerky left. She'd just started to turn when the chilling wind on the back of her neck turned hot and sticky.

She knew without turning that Wildman stood behind her.

17

Grabbed from behind. It happened so fast that she didn't have time to react. She kicked wildly and fought with what little strength she had left. But she couldn't nail her target.

"Get away from me!"

Another noise, the sound of footsteps crushing brush. "Cody, stop! Don't fight him!"

"Derek!" Cody's fists lashed out aimlessly as Wildman's arms tightened around her. "Derek!" she cried over her shoulder. "Help me!"

She could smell Wildman. Actually smell the dirty stink of his unbathed body. It made her want to puke.

"Let go!" she screamed again.

"Don't fight him, Cody!" Derek sounded as desperate as she felt. "You're making it worse!"

Wildman pinned her arms to her side. She struggled as sweat dripped in her eyes, stinging as before. She couldn't wipe them. Her shouts died to whimpers. *Save your breath.* Her kicks fell to pathetic shuffles. *Save your energy.* Her whole body went limp.

"It's okay," Derek said. "You can let her go."

It sounded as if Derek was telling Wildman what to do. Wildman's reply was a grunt, followed by mumblings from the Tlingit woman, who must have been nearby.

"Cody?" Derek said again. "We'll let you go if you promise not to run away."

We?

"Cody. Are you listening?"

Maybe Derek had been brainwashed. She'd heard about kidnappers brainwashing their victims.

"He's going to let you go, okay?"

Giving in was her only chance to get away. "Okay."

When Wildman released her she whirled around. Wildman sank back, his dark eyes disappearing in the shadows. Cody stepped back just as quickly, letting the damp air wash over her—all the while glancing from Derek to Wildman and back to Derek.

Neither Cody nor Derek said anything for what seemed like an eternity. Then she drew him into a hug. "You okay?" she asked.

Derek hugged her back; she felt his nod against her cheek.

She turned toward Wildman, who had moved to the clearing by the fire. The woman was looking away and watching them at the same time.

"What happened to your leg?" Derek asked, studying Cody again.

"Who cares about my leg?" She wanted to shake Derek out of whatever hold these people had on him. *"Let's get out of here!"* she mouthed, then grabbed his hand and tried to pull him. But he pulled back.

"It isn't what you think," he said.

It's okay, she wanted to say. *You can tell me about it later. When we're back on the water, safely on our way.*

"I had to go with them. It was the only way, and I knew you wouldn't come with me, with him. You were convinced he was a poacher. And we needed help, Cody. We couldn't do it by ourselves. One kayak. No food. The rising water. Everything."

Derek talked in half thoughts, making no sense at all. But he *looked* okay. Thinner, but not in a bad way. Just all tucked up like an athlete. His peeling skin had tanned over. And he was clean—that alone was a miracle. Even his hair had a scrubbed luster.

If someone saw the two of them standing in the trees under a sky of buttermilk clouds, he'd think Cody was the one who needed help. Her body was emaciated. No doubt her eyes had that hollow sunken look and were probably rimmed with dark circles. Her clothes were torn and matted with mud and blood.

"I had to do something," he was saying. "Since I tore up the note."

Cody stiffened when Wildman moved; he slipped inside the shack and closed the door. (He must have circled behind her earlier, when she'd first spotted the smoke.) His smell lingered in the trees.

Then she realized with revulsion that the stink had been hers all along.

Derek stared at her. "Cody?"

The icy breeze slapped through her tattered clothes. She took a step back, then another. Then she turned and took off running. Cody cut one way, slipped, caught herself before going all the way down, and kept moving.

Suddenly she had understood what he was telling her. Derek had gone with them willingly.

"Wait up!" Derek called after her.

She could feel him catching up to her. "You weren't kidnapped?" she cried over her shoulder.

Without warning he tackled her and she went down, wincing as pain shot through her leg. She scrambled to crawl away, but he was so much stronger. Rested and fueled.

He flipped her over as he used to when they had wrestled. "I knew you'd follow us. We waited and watched for you on the trail. Mary Jane slept near you last night to make sure you were safe. She waited until you got up this morning so we knew you were on the right trail."

Cody tried to kick free but it was impossible. "How could you trust poachers?"

"It isn't like that—" Derek began.

She cut him off. "He cut my kayak loose. Now he has both of us here. No kayak, no food. I'll bet the other kayak is long gone. And he knows it's impossible for us to hike back to Yakutat."

Derek's expression changed, softening. "You're wrong. He didn't cut the kayak. He *found* it. That's how he knew someone needed help."

Finally Derek rolled off her and stood up.

Cody scrambled to her feet. "We don't need his help." She was close to crying now, hating herself for it. "Didn't you hear the chopper? The rescue party knows we're here. They spotted our camp. They'll be coming back."

Derek shook his head slowly. "The chopper wasn't looking for us."

Cody searched his face for answers. "What are you talking about?"

She stood her ground while he spun out another story, this time explaining away the helicopter. Hubbard Glacier. There were all kinds of media there: TV news crews, newspaper reporters, environmentalists and geologists, all camped on the banks across from the massive plug of ice that had closed off the mouth of the fjord. A few small planes had actually landed on the outwash plains bordering the glacier; helicopters had lowered photographers onto the frozen river.

She listened quietly, keeping an eye on the trees lining the clearing, in case Wildman decided to come back. "How do you know all this?"

"Eric canoed that part of the fjord earlier in the week," he said. "He hiked up on a ridge and watched them all afternoon."

"Eric?" She figured he meant Wildman. "If he really wanted to help, he would've told someone about us."

Derek turned and started back to the clearing. "They're helping us by giving us food and gear. And Eric rescued your kayak. Now we have two."

Cody found herself trailing Derek slowly through the trees, toward the clearing. The woman was at the fire cutting a fleshy root into the steaming pot. It looked like skunk cabbage. A hunk of meat was added next, some kind of bloodred animal with a thick layer of fat.

Cody hated herself, but the meat was the most beautiful sight she'd ever seen.

Sun filtered though the trees, bathing the wet ground with a glowing red aura. The red glow made the landscape look as if the world were on fire. Or maybe it was coming to an end.

Cody sank to an old log, exhausted. She needed time to think about everything Derek had just told her.

18

The trees were a steep canyon showing only a sliver of hard blue sky. In seconds the sliver turned from blue to white, changing with the whim of the wind and clouds. Old-man's beard hung from the highest limbs. The gray moss was as deadly as a parasite, though it didn't steal nutrients from its victims; it simply smothered them. Back in California it killed hordes of oak trees.

The wind blew harder still.

Drops began to fall. They splatted No Fear. No matter. It could use a good washing. So could she.

The woman joined Wildman, slipping inside the hut.

Moments before, Derek had retreated to the fire. He'd left her, saying "They're okay, Cody. I wouldn't lie. They aren't poachers. Those skins we saw in the cabin were beaver, hunted legally over a whole season. You can go back to our camp if you want, but I'm not going with you. I'm going all the way to Hubbard."

Cody hadn't asked Derek about the Tlingit woman. Cody hadn't asked a lot of things. There was too much to absorb. If Wildman wasn't a threat, then why the mask?

Part of Derek's story made sense. Newscasters and geologists would have flocked to Hubbard Glacier to check out such a monumental event. The day before she had even wondered where the save-the-whale activists were.

Now she knew they were at Hubbard. Flying in from Yakutat on the ocean side. Except for the lone helicopter that had flown down the fjord, for some unknown reason. She still believed that if Wildman wanted to help them he could have told the people at Hubbard where they were.

Derek sat alone by the fire, his shoulders sagging.

She couldn't believe she and Derek were on opposite sides of the fence, each trying to convince the other to make the long climb over.

A raindrop hit her face, then two. Not a single sizzle in the fire; the sky was spitting at her alone. Part of her wanted to believe everything Derek had said. But another voice kept saying, *Be careful. Something isn't right here.* Not talking to outsiders. The mask. It gave her the creeps. She knew what the outfitters said about people who lived in the woods. "They're usually hiding from something."

The dark-haired woman backed slowly out of the hut; Wildman remained inside. A thick necklace of shells adorned the woman's chest, the same type of shells that decorated her poncho and mukluks. She moved to the fire and whispered something to Derek.

Derek nodded, then made his way to the trees where he'd left Cody. "Eric knows you're afraid of him," he said. "He promises to stay in the shelter so that you can warm up by the fire." Derek's eyes begged her to follow him to the clearing. "We can paddle to Hubbard anytime, Cody. We're not prisoners. But first you have to eat something and rest."

From behind his back Derek held up a hunk of meat. Meat! Dripping with greasy fat, attached to a bundle of ribs. Spareribs! Of venison, probably. She hesitated; then something took over and she grabbed the bundle of bones and dropped to a mossy boulder, hard and cold. She gnawed on the meat like an animal. Fat saturated her hands, dripped off her chin. Nothing had ever tasted so good.

"Not so fast," he said. "You'll get sick."

Cody didn't care. She couldn't stop herself. Her stomach demanded every greasy, stringy tendon. With eyes closed, she swallowed half-chewed chunks and gagged. Chewing seemed such a waste of time. She didn't even feel bad about eating a deer. It wasn't like swallowing the gull's unborn chicks.

"How far is it to Hubbard?" she asked, teeth working on the bones, stripping them stark white in places, bloodred in others.

Derek glanced at the shelter before he answered. "About six hours by kayak."

The glance meant *Wildman says it's that far.*

Six hours! It couldn't be more than ten in the morning, eleven at the latest. Paddling together, the two of them could make it in one day. *Today.* She was sure of it. Her mother would be out of her mind with worry by now.

Cody wiped her mouth on her sleeve, adding grease to the rest of the mess. *Six hours*, she thought. How many days had they paddled down the fjord? Two. Plus the day hiking yesterday. So three days traveling. Five altogether but some of that was at the second camp when her eyes had been sunburned. "No way. We can't be that close."

Derek took the cleaned bones and tossed them into the woods. "The trail cut off a bunch of twisting and turning in the fjord," he said.

Cody eyed the hut. "Then why does he have to go with us?"

"I already told you he doesn't."

She hadn't remembered that.

"You know we couldn't have made it, Cody," he said.

Her stomach grumbled and rolled over as if it wasn't sure what to do with so much meat and grease. Being so full surprised it; she hadn't thought she'd ever be full again. Cleaning off the last bone, she stuck it in her hip pocket. She wasn't sure why, but it was a good fit.

She still couldn't get used to seeing Derek in the animal skin poncho. "Why does he wear that mask? And what are they doing out here?"

Derek's face clouded over. "I can't tell you."

"Then you know."

He nodded.

The wind picked up, making sounds like tribal chanting in the forest. Another gust carried high-pitched singing. Her mind was playing tricks on her. Too many hours had passed since she'd been dry and warm.

"Mary Jane, his wife, she'll tell you."

"Why can't you tell me?"

"It isn't my story to tell. But she'll tell you—she told me."

Derek looked down at the wet leaves on his boots. She'd never seen him act like this before. He glanced at the fire and said, "Come over to the fire and dry out, and let Mary Jane look at your leg."

Cody knew she had to dry off and rest. Just a thirty-minute nap and she'd be good for another hundred miles. But nobody was going to touch her leg, she told Derek. And she wasn't going near Wildman.

Her pack held a T-shirt and shorts. Not much else. But she couldn't take off her tights since they were stuck to her scab. She'd change right where she was under the shelter of the trees. "Can I use your sleeping bag? Mine is wet."

Derek headed back to the clearing and gathered up his sleeping bag, a thick fur blanket, and a pot of cooled water. She couldn't believe how well he fit into this scene.

I won't go to sleep, just close my eyes for a while, she thought after she'd taken off her boots, changed her clothes and slipped into the dry, warm bag. The fur blanket turned out to be a good ground cover, keeping the dampness from filtering up.

Derek had brought over a wool poncho too, similar to the woman's but without shells. Cody let the poncho stay where it was: hanging on a broken limb.

I'm only going to close my eyes for a few minutes, she told herself.

Soon she dozed, then slept hard.

Hours later she bolted up with a start when something told her she wasn't merely dreaming about a nonhuman creature. There was one next to her in the dark. She didn't know where she was, didn't know what was happening. She did know it was blackout dark and a huge shape of something hulky was nearby.

Cody ripped her way out of the bag, suddenly remembering that she was in the Alaskan wilderness. *Wildman*. She thrashed through the underbrush but didn't get far, stubbing her toe on something blunt. She cried out in pain and, in the glint of a waning moon, saw the Tlingit woman rise off the boulder and move toward her.

19

The woman stopped in the moonlight filtering through a break in the trees. Except for the wavering glow from the fire, everything else sank back in the dark shadows.

"What do you want?" Cody whispered, wondering if Wildman had kept his word and stayed in the shelter. Then she smelled that stench and realized she hadn't even cleaned up before crawling into the sleeping bag.

I must have conked out for hours.

The woman didn't answer.

Something sleek winked at Cody from the ground near her feet. The bear horn must have rolled out of the sleeping bag. That was what she'd stubbed her toe on. Cody was surprised it hadn't sounded off.

"What do you want?" she repeated.

Finally the woman answered. "Are you hungry?"

Starving was more like it.

"Uh, no."

"Thirsty, then?"

The woman had a kind voice, soft and warm.

"No, thank you."

"There is nothing to fear. My husband sleeps in our fishing shelter alongside your cousin."

Cody couldn't imagine Wildman and Derek sleeping side by side.

"Even if he was here beside me you would have nothing to fear. Come, sit by the fire. I have made a poultice for your wound. And there is vegetable stew left from last night's dinner."

Dinner? Judging by the chill seeping through Cody's bones, it must be two or three A.M. She was hardly aware of the surrounding dampness. The cold was becoming an old friend.

The woman said, "Come. It's no good to be so cold and dirty."

Her words carried a hint of an accent. Cody realized it was the careful way in which she laid down her words that gave them their rhythm, soft and resonant like a distant bell.

Cody surprised herself by following the woman to the fire. She knew the door to the fishing shelter could creak open at any moment. Still she stayed by the fire, only a few feet from the shelter and its rawhide-lashed door. If Wildman had wanted to hurt her, he would have done it before now.

The steam off the hot-water-soaked cloth and the warmth of the fire felt luxurious. She held the cloth to her face until sweat and mud dripped and the cloth cooled. The woman replaced it with a second steaming cloth, then peeled the socks from Cody's feet and lifted them to a sudsy pot. Cody winced as heat awoke her half-numb toes; then heat finally won out and the pain subsided.

"It will be ten years this winter since the accident," the woman said.

Cody knew she meant Wildman.

The woman was going to tell his story.

"An expedition to Mount McKinley. Denali is the Indian name. It is the highest mountain in North America. More than twenty thousand feet."

Cody nodded.

"My husband was an experienced high-altitude guide, and he led others over the most treacherous route to the summit of Denali. This route required technical climbing, with ropes and ice axes, and crampons buckled over boots.

"It takes more than a month to make such a journey, so all food and provisions had to be carried with them, packed on sleds and dragged over the ice like a team of sled dogs instead of men."

The woman paused and stared into the fire. The flickering light danced in her eyes, adding to her quiet beauty. Then she continued, "The mountain is an icebound graveyard; the peak itself is a gravestone. Yet many are compelled to try to conquer it, not knowing that the mountain will demand a sacrifice in return.

"Traveling over ice fields and glaciers, each man was tied to the next in case he plummeted into a crevasse. The sleds were also tied with sturdy climbing rope, linked like deadweights between them. If the line to the sled wasn't held tight, the sled could fall into a crevasse on top of the man in front of it and crush him.

"My husband fell through ice no fewer than seven times, but the man behind him always held the sled line tight so that the sled never called him for the sacrifice."

Cody listened intently, hardly aware that her feet had been slipped into a pair of fur boots much like those the woman wore. The insides were sheepskin, like her Ugg boots back home. Her tights had been slit with a knife, the wound cleaned and dressed with a fresh bandage.

"Then the storm came. It was completely dark at ten in the morning. The wind blew sideways at sixty miles per hour, knocking the men off their feet. It was colder than forty degrees below zero for many, many hours. Holding the sled line straight and stiff in the face of such a storm is how my husband lost three fingers on his right hand."

Cody shivered, unable to imagine such bitterly cold conditions. Wildman's gloves were worn to hide missing fingers.

The woman tucked a blanket around Cody's shoulders and placed a cup of stew in her hands. Cody smiled a silent thank-you. Then she sipped the hot liquid, swirled it in her mouth, sloshed it over her teeth, and swallowed. The stew warmed her from the inside out.

"They huddled on an icy slope for hours, shouting and hitting one another to keep awake. For a brief spell the clouds broke and stars shone through. My husband urged everyone onward, to find a safe camp for the night. But one man had untied himself from the rope. High altitude and little oxygen make people do crazy things. He stepped off the mountain, and was lost.

"My husband was the leader. He untied himself and climbed down after the man, and then *he* was lost. The tradition says to leave the dead on the mountain, like sailors who are buried at sea. The others thought that my husband was dead, so they left him. Another expedition found him and brought him back, but he'd lost his nose and much of his cheeks."

The mask was to protect an ice-scarred face.

Derek had been right. Wildman—*Eric*—was trying to save them from the same fate as the man he'd lost on the mountain. If only she'd known.

"Since that time we have lived a subsistence life, alone in the woods except for a yearly journey into Yakutat to visit my family and trade for luxuries, such as fishing line and toothpaste. But the dead man haunts my husband still. That is all there is to tell," the woman said, standing up in the predawn light. "Come, it is time to catch fish for breakfast."

Cody felt warm in the poncho and fur boots. Too warm and, strangely, too safe. She felt guilty for being clean and well fed and so utterly comfortable in this raw untamed wilderness. She glanced back at the shelter before trailing the woman and her two fishing poles down a path to the water's edge.

She felt bad about many things, good about many others.

20

Only the eerie fugue of wind and water broke the stillness around Cody and Mary Jane. They made an odd-looking fishing couple on the bank of a meltwater stream that drained into the fjord.

At first the sight of the fjord had surprised Cody; she hadn't had any idea the fishing shelter was this close to shore. All that winding around on the trail had cut miles off the water route, a shortcut that put them closer to Hubbard, as Derek had said. She'd choked up at the sight of her kayak tied to a tree, the deep blue canvas-covered craft bobbing in perfect sync with the rising water.

She finally turned to Mary Jane, embarrassed by her curiosity but still needing to know. "What happened to the rest of the men in the expedition?"

Mary Jane raised her face to the east, embracing the rising sun. "We have spoken enough about the dead. It is now best to care for the living."

And Cody understood that they were buried in some icebound grave.

With enough fish to feed four people, they slogged back to camp in the face of biting winds. Derek knelt by the fire, straining to shove his sleeping bag into its stuff sack. The daypacks lay open on the ground, awaiting supplies to be carried through the day's journey.

Derek had changed back into rubber boots and a rain slicker and looked almost normal, except for the lost weight, the untamed hair, and the calm in his voice. "Breakfast?" he asked, unmoved by Cody's new wardrobe.

"Yeah."

Mary Jane took the fish from the twig stringer and wrapped them whole in large leaves, pushing them into the ashes—all without regard to the shelter door, which remained closed.

Cody finally said, "He doesn't need to stay inside."

Derek glanced at the shelter before speaking up. "Eric isn't here. He hiked back to our camp, for the tent and the other kayak."

Cody was disappointed. She wanted Wildman to know she wasn't afraid of him and understood about the mask.

Derek misread her expression as worry about getting back on the water. "It won't take him long."

"My husband knows the fjord better than the otters," Mary Jane said, looking at the sky for a hint of sun behind the lightest clouds. "One hour more, maybe."

They ate the whole fish in silence, picking the steaming meat from the loose skin and saving the bones. The early morning passed quickly with the chores of washing up after breakfast and preparing a sack lunch for a day away. The sack was a tanned deerskin pouch. The lunch was venison and fish jerky dried for the winter and the last of the fresh huckleberries, glossy and black.

"I will make another poultice for your wound from the root of devil's club. It is part of the ginseng family," Mary Jane said, taking a brush to Cody's hair. She brushed it smooth, gathered it into a braid, and tied it with yarn. "You will take the poultice with you."

"Thanks," Cody said, though she was hardly limping. Long before sunset, still more than fifteen hours away, she and Derek would be safe and warm inside Yakutat Lodge, their mothers fussing over their every need. At Hubbard, one of the helicopters or a bush plane would fly them back. The day really would be marked *The End*.

Cody spent too much time with every chore, as if she were in the last chapter of a good novel and didn't want to turn the final pages. The day before, if someone had told her she'd be sorry to see an end to this story, she would have said he was crazy.

Down at the water's edge she loaded her kayak, talking to it as she worked, as if she were renewing an old friendship. She finally gave up the fur mukluks and wool poncho in exchange for her boots and rain slicker. The rubber felt like cold steel against her skin, and out of place here. Her dance tights were little more than shreds but helped keep the bandage in place on her wound.

Mary Jane scooped rainwater from a large yellow-cedar canoe, handcarved like those that had belonged to her ancestors thirty-five-hundred years ago. The smile in her eyes said Wildman had come into view.

Cody took in the sight: A man with a wild beard and a mass of white-streaked hair guided the kayak with broad, powerful strokes. The craft responded effortlessly and without a single ripple at the bow.

Wildman didn't come anywhere near her. Instead he steered to the shallow water next to Derek and handed him the bowline. Then Wildman trudged up the rocky bank and disappeared in the shadows of the trees.

Cody had just settled into her kayak when Mary Jane removed her shell necklace and placed it over Cody's head. Cody fingered the smooth white shells, searching for special words, something more than thank you. When nothing came, she simply said, "Thank you," meaning it with all her heart.

Mary Jane smiled her words. "It is you who brought the gift."

Cody smiled back and squeezed her hand.

Before snapping down the rubber skirt, Cody spotted bubbles seeping through a slit in the bottom of her kayak.

"What is it?" Derek asked, one boot inside his wobbly craft.

"A hole in the canvas," she said. "It's small, so it should be okay for one more day."

Mary Jane steadied the kayak with her strong hands. "There is no such thing as a small leak," she said. "My husband will repair it for you. First we must remove your kayak from the water."

Derek tied his kayak and started clearing a space near shore. Rocks, driftwood, and other debris were tossed in a pile. Mary Jane used a flat rock to dig a long groove in the damp earth.

"Should we unload first?" Cody asked.

"What for?" Derek said, already swinging the kayak's bow onto land.

A gust of wind lifted the hem of Cody's slicker as she stepped into the icy water. She balanced carefully on the slippery rocks, making her way to the stern. With Mary Jane helping Derek at the bow and Cody pushing on the rear, the kayak slowly slid into the cleared area.

They maneuvered the kayak until it was sideways over the long groove. Mary Jane fingered the slit: a clean cut and less than a half inch long. "This can be mended from the inside," she said, scooping out the offending water. Then she called to her husband.

Cody glanced up when Eric ambled down the embankment. She quickly looked away, not wanting him to think she was staring. She followed his movements from the corner of her eye. He knelt on the other side of the kayak and opened a pouch. Inside, freshly cut wild grass spilled out, and a fist-sized wad of an amber-colored object.

Cody didn't want to stare but the mask drew her gaze. She wanted to speak so he'd know that she wasn't afraid. She longed to tell him she was sorry about the accident. But her thoughts kept turning into questions about his face. Instead she looked away.

Where trees had blown down, sunlight trickled through and opened the forest floor to a maze of grasses and wildflowers, vital prewinter food for wildlife. At the mouth of these streams and rivers, salt and fresh waters usually mixed, stirred twice daily by ocean tides. But that was no longer the case, not since a seventy-mile river of ice had slid across the opening at Disenchantment Bay.

Derek picked up a knife with a hand-hewn handle and antler blade. "How are we going to repair the hole?"

"Tree sap," Eric replied. His words were nearly smothered by the mask, so he was hard to understand. "We'll make a patch."

Cody was startled by the sound of his voice. "How long will it take?" she asked quickly. It came out sounding as if she couldn't wait to get away.

Eric's eyes smiled kindly over his mask. "Not long."

Mary Jane rose, and the shells on her mukluks played a tune. "We need something to eat while we work."

Eric passed a wad of sap to Derek. "From a pine tree," he said. "Chew it until it's soft."

Cody held out her palm. "I'll take some."

Cody and Derek chewed while Eric spread the cut grass on a flat rock. Cody kept looking at Eric, looking away, then looking back. Eric cut off a piece of sap for himself, but turned his head before slipping it under the mask and into his mouth.

The wind blew from the north, whipping off ice fields and glaciers, promising subfreezing temperatures in the coming days. Waves churned by the wind rolled onshore, several feet from the kayak. Something would have to give in the fjord; the water couldn't rise forever.

Cody tried imagining winter in Southeast Alaska, the boughs of conifers keeping snow off the ground directly beneath trees, making it easier for deer and other animals to forage for scarce winter food. No wonder the forest was so thick. The constant dampness prevented natural fires from lightning strikes, the kind that swept through the interior forests, and those in California.

"Is Hubbard ever going to recede?" Cody studied Eric's eyes for an answer.

"The water pressure is building up." Eric turned his head to remove his wad, then worked it like putty into the hole with a gloved finger. The sap hardened instantly in the cold. "Soon water will burst through the ice dam."

Cody added her softened sap to a mixture of grass and sand. Derek used the knife to spread it over the first layer.

Mary Jane brought a basket of berries, salmon jerky, and a gourd of tea steeped from herbs. Derek dug into the food. "I'm starving."

Cody took a piece of jerky for later, then passed

the basket to Eric, who shook his head. "I ate on the water."

She figured he didn't want to eat in front of them.

The others ate berries while Eric poured cold water over the patch to harden it. "A person's weight will be the true test," he said, dragging the kayak down to the water.

Cody followed him. She wanted to tell him she was sorry for all the terrible things she had thought about him. "I am happy to have known you," she wanted to say.

Eric was leaning into the kayak with his body weight, watching for any water that might seep in.

Cody hesitated; suddenly her throat tightened up. All the things she wanted to say sounded too much like good-bye. Instead she touched the shell necklace and asked if the leak was fixed. Slowly her hand dropped from the shells and found its way to his shoulder. "I'm sorry," she whispered.

21

Out in the fjord, under skies opaque with clouds and drizzle, Cody shook hands with her paddle for the first time in almost a week. She threw her shoulders into her strokes, skimming the water away from shore, paddling toward Derek, who was already pointed in the direction of Hubbard. "Think we can remember how to do this?" she called to him.

Derek nodded. His face was a twist of mixed emotions; then it relaxed into a smile. "Same old friends. Paddle and water."

"It's another world." She felt just as bad about leaving, but for different reasons: Eric had saved their lives but she hadn't thanked him the way she had wanted to.

Cody looked back at Eric and Mary Jane, who stood on shore, their gazes fixed on the two kayaks. Cody raised her paddle in a final farewell. Eric slowly lifted his gloved hand and returned the gesture.

Then they were off.

The cool moist air was misty as always. No wonder this part of the world produced such lush forests, an extension of the rain belt of the Pacific Northwest, a sanctuary for both animals and men. Even under over-cast skies she could tell that the sun was declaring it to be midmorning.

Since first light came at four A.M., a person could have a full life before noon. The drizzle turned to light rain. They were warm enough in their rain gear with the rubber skirts snapped down. Mary Jane had packed enough jerky and berries to put fat reserves on a grizzly.

The lonely ice-armored ranges looked down on a hostile coast with steep, scarred rock: There was no relief in this part of the fjord, no place to hole up if they had to. Another sweeping bend, and the mouth of a canyon displayed a fan-shaped bank, a tiny creek flowing through it. Alaska yellow cedars were only small trees in the swampy soil studded with ferns, so richly green in places they took your breath away.

Derek finally broke the silence. "I'm going back."

At first she thought he meant paddle back to the fishing shelter. "What do you mean?"

"They spend every summer at the shelter. I'm going back next year. Stay a couple of weeks. Learn about fishing and trapping. Maybe I'll spend the whole summer."

"What will you tell your mom?" Cody asked, timing her strokes with her breathing.

Derek shouted over the rising wind. "We can't tell anyone about Eric and Mary Jane."

Cody nodded. "I know."

"But I know what happened and I have the map," he said. "That's enough for me."

An hour farther into the fjord the clouds broke loose with heavy, bitter rain. The mountains spouted waterfalls—more fuel to the ever-rising fjord. Cody tightened her hood, realizing she'd left her baseball cap behind. No Fear. Someday an archaeologist would discover it along with the remains of primitive fishing gear.

Her paddle strained in the face of stabbing rain; streams in the distance were swollen and raging. The fjord flooded all around the kayak. Although her mind told her they were fine as long as they were on the water, her heart pounded.

Rain slashed at them for another hour before it lightened to a swirling mist. She threw back her hood and breathed easier. The Tlingits had explored, hunted, fished, and claimed the lands and waters as their own as far back as ten thousand years before, when the glaciers began receding. For thousands of years the region had survived ice, floods, earthquakes, and fires. Yet one event had created a lake overnight.

Derek skimmed the water alongside Cody. "Thanks," he said simply.

She studied him, still paddling. "What for?"

"For bringing me out here."

"We came through for each other," she said, remembering her snow blindness. "When it counted most."

A flock of surf scoters landed on the water near the kayaks. "Nothing will ever be the same," said Derek, eyes on the birds. "Everything is different."

Cody knew what he meant. They were different

because of all they'd been through. "Do you know what the outfitters call an adventure?"

"What?"

"An experience outside your comfort zone," she said.

Derek smiled. "We had an adventure, Cody."

Cody heard the *whap, whap, whap* of rotary blades. Like a metal insect, a helicopter appeared down the fjord, moving steadily toward the kayaks. The kayaks floated silently as the helicopter zipped down the middle of the canyon. The sound was unbelievably loud and out of place.

Derek lowered his paddle. "Do they know who we are?"

Cody tucked her braid into her slicker and slumped against the artificial wind and noise. The man riding shotgun was in a khaki uniform, a forest ranger, probably. He waved and pressed a thumbs-up to the dome window; then the chopper spun in a tight arch and buzzed back to Hubbard.

"I guess so," she said.

22

All the days, all the miles, all the twists and turns in the fjord and in herself couldn't have prepared Cody for the sight of Hubbard Glacier blocking the mouth of Disenchantment Bay. A massive ice cork shoved into Gilbert Point on the west; the glacial dam itself a twenty-six-story skyscraper rising above a layer of fresh water that capped the deeper salt water.

She was vaguely aware of bits and pieces of civilization off to the sides, a scant five miles away. Dome tents were but mere dots atop Gilbert Point; on the northeast side, across from the point, bush planes littering an ancient river of dried mud and debris. And a single helicopter, its blades still whirling. Most likely the same chopper that had buzzed them earlier.

Ant-sized people rushed down to the water near the airstrip, arms raised and waving wildly. Probably shouting too. Nothing could be heard above the din of water and wind.

They're waving at us, she realized. *They're calling to us!*

She looked over at Derek, who'd stopped paddling, his face thin under the yellow hood, his dark eyes taking it all in. Culture shock. It was just too much. He seemed lost—which was odd since they were *found*.

Derek looked back at her and a shared feeling passed between them. For a few more minutes they would be bound with water and weather and the fjord. She remembered how she had sworn at the elements, cursed at them for plotting and scheming against her. Now the word *respect* had worked its way into her mind.

As they silently paddled, Cody thought about her mother back in the tavern, receiving word from the chopper. With one call the unbearable burden of worry would crumble and drop away. She pictured her mother on the tarmac of Yakutat's one-strip airport, huddled against the wind, waiting.

An explosive crackling and roaring reverberated through the fjord as an ice cliff three hundred fifty feet high calved from Hubbard's face. The cliff disappeared under its own cloud of spray, then vaulted up into the air seconds later, careened forward, and shoved a giant wall of water at the kayaks. Mother Nature wasn't about to let them go without a fight.

The kayaks offered no security, and shore was too far away to reach in time. Explosions of other calving bergs boomed across the fjord as the wall of churning foam and ice bore down on them.

Cody yelled, "Get ready!" and gripped her paddle as though born with it. She braced herself as the onrush washed over and into her kayak, and she was drenched to the skin one more time.

She saw Derek's face—all smiles—just a paddle

length away, hollering, *"Yee ha!"* like a bronco rider. Then he dropped, disappearing in a watery trough. Only a scrap of blue canvas showed as he was swept sideways into a deeper hole: Cody's kayak plunged headlong into the second hole, then flipped. No time to hold her breath. No time to hold anything.

Except her paddle.

Always her paddle.

In the middle of a split-second roll, ice picks stabbed at her body, which numbed almost immediately. Just as quickly the torrent rolled the kayak all the way over and spit it into the air. It was over that fast. She breathed hard, her chest on fire and numb at the same time. Her head throbbed with the pain of cold. She couldn't hear a sound. Cody released her death grip on the paddle to touch her ears and be sure they were still there.

Frantically she searched the swells for Derek. *Where was he?*

Then she spotted his kayak, miles away it seemed, but probably only a hundred feet, bucking the white-caps—upside down.

Derek was awash in the fjord.

She paddled like a crazy person, screaming, "Hang on!", faintly aware of the *whap* of blades in the distance.

He's going to die, she thought. *Like the men in Wildman's expedition. Glaciers demand a human sacrifice. Just like mountains.*

Then she swore loud and clear, mad as anything that she'd forgiven the elements so soon.

If it hadn't been for the flash of his orange life vest she wouldn't have been able to see Derek at all. She paddled wildly, slashing the water in an incredible display of what could be accomplished when someone was scared out of her mind.

The helicopter buzzed in front of her, hovering over the water, a cigar-shaped float swaying on the end of a rope. Derek swiped at it uselessly. Too much wind, too much water.

She closed the final yards, grabbing the nape of the orange vest, dragging Derek, coughing and sputtering, over the seat behind her. Except for the hood, which had been torn off, the rain slicker remained intact; but his boots had been stripped away, exposing feet as blue as Hubbard. Looking lifeless, he still managed to crawl all the way in. Then he collapsed nearly unconscious, stone-white fingers gripping the canvas lip. No time to dig out the sleeping bag. No time for anything but to react to what was happening.

"Hang on!" she shouted over the roar of exploding ice. "That's an order from your captain!"

A hint of a smile tinged his pale blue lips, then faded as he sank into unconsciousness.

23

ody's mind went numb as sleeping bags appeared from nowhere, doubling as blankets, wrapping her and Derek like mummies. *Faces.* A horde of them crowding around her on the muddy shore, battering her with questions. A mass of jumbled syllables that made no sense. So much noise. She realized how conversation between them had steadily dwindled since they had first left the pickup. Something else had taken over.

These people were so unbelievably clean. And Derek. A man in a khaki uniform was rushing him off to the helicopter. Trailed by Aunt Jessie. *Aunt Jessie?*

Cody accepted a mug of something hot with trembling hands. Coffee. Black. She hated and loved it at the same time. *Aunt Jessie? At Hubbard?* The coffee warmed both her hands and her insides, finally thawing the numbness in her head. *Of course. Flown in from Yakutat, less than an hour away by plane.*

In a shroud of confusion she wondered where they were taking Derek and why she wasn't going. She must have thought aloud, since bits and pieces filtered in. "Not enough room in the helicopter . . . Don't worry, he's going to be okay . . . landing pad on the

hospital roof . . . another chopper on the way . . .''
More than anything she wanted to be with her cousin.

Then an unmistakable cry: "Cody!"

She wrapped herself tightly with the sleeping bag, spilling hot coffee all over the place, realizing she was seated on the bow of her kayak, having been pulled ashore only moments before by these strangers.

Cody scanned the muddy airstrip for the voice, searching the faces milling around. Then the faces blurred into the background as her mother, bundled against the icy cold, came into focus, slogging through the heavy mud near a small plane with its propellers still spinning. And Patterson, bent over to shelter Mom from the raw wind. All the way from California.

Mom and Patterson pushed quickly through the crowd and pulled Cody into a hug, crying and soothing her. "Are you okay?" And, over and over again, "We love you!"

She tried to talk, to answer, to say, "I love you too," but they hushed her, told her to save her strength, and hugged her even tighter. She mumbled, "I lost my cap. No Fear." Then she heard Patterson laugh. How she loved his laugh! She'd missed him so much. She clung to them both, never wanting to let go.

She closed her eyes and remembered all of it from the moment they'd sneaked off with the old pickup to battling the icebergs, but mostly the early morning by the fire when Mary Jane had told her the story about the expedition on Denali. Cody touched her shells, making sure the necklace was still intact. It was.

Suddenly she knew he was there too. When she looked over her mother's shoulder she wasn't surprised to see her father. Huddled in a parka, the hood framing his moist eyes. Looking lost and scared and sad all at once. Something inside her said, *Go to him. Tell him it's okay.*

Comfort him, at least. That's what a caring person would do.

She wanted to, tried to move even, but couldn't.

Without looking at him she knew he was coming toward her. She sensed him moving slowly, as if he were treading on black ice. She felt him touch her braid, stroke her hair the way he used to. *Turn to him. You can let him hug you. Give him a break, Cody! It's been three years!*

They hugged in silence as ice tumbled into the water and spray erupted hundreds of feet in the air. Gulls swooped down to feed on brine shrimp swirling on the surface. A cloud drifted from the sun's path long enough to bring shadows to life, illuminating brilliant shades of blue.

Still no one spoke.

All too soon the familiar sound of rotary blades buzzed over the glacier, overpowering both the sound of cracking ice and her thoughts.

Dad released her from the hug.

Cody stepped off the bow with Patterson's help. "No Fear?" he said. "You didn't lose it, Cody."

Mom held her close as she tried to stand; Dad gathered the sleeping bag so that it wouldn't drag in the mud.

It didn't seem right that Derek wasn't here with her. Then with one last look at Hubbard she smiled a farewell, feeling sad in a way she didn't fully understand. She embraced the icy wind stinging her cheeks and took her first step in the mud soup toward the waiting helicopter.

Author's Note

In the summer of 1994, I joined a kayaking expedition in Russell Fjord Wilderness Area, at the northern tip of Southeast Alaska. The goal of our journey was to paddle the length of the fjord, reaching the largest tidewater glacier in North America: Hubbard Glacier.

The long daylight hours of Alaska's summer coaxed us mile after mile down the windswept saltwater passage, cloaked in a constant drizzle. Evenings I huddled in my tent under the spell of the fjord's geological and social history, devouring every bit of printed matter carried by our guides.

In the spring of 1986 one of Hubbard's tributary glaciers began surging as much as 130 feet a day. The action spurred Hubbard into a rapid state of advancement, pushing a plug of mud and rock against the opposite shore. The mouth of the fjord was closed off, creating the world's largest glacier-formed lake.

The idea for *Frozen Stiff* came at two in the morning when I was awakened by water seeping into my tent. I jokingly remarked, "Maybe Hubbard has surged again and Disenchantment Bay is blocked off. Maybe the water in the fjord is rising the way it did in 1986." Back then, an eighty-foot layer of fresh water, an accumulation of rain, glacial melt, and rivers, floated atop the salt water. Fish, seals, and porpoises were trapped inside the newly formed lake.

I was quickly assured by our guide that our rising

water was caused by the high tide. But my mind was already spinning with *what if*'s? What if two kids had been kayaking in the fjord when Hubbard surged? What if they'd lost most of their food and supplies on the swelling water? What if no one knew they were there?

The dilapidated fishing hut in *Frozen Stiff* can still be seen in Russell Fjord, surrounded by native wildflowers and stately conifers. But the ice dam blocking Disenchantment Bay burst four months after it formed, sending more than 3.5 million cubic feet of outflow per second gushing from the fjord. The force was thirty-five times the flow of Niagara Falls, pouring out at thirty-five miles an hour.

Unlike Cody and Derek in the story, our group managed to complete the journey without flipping our kayaks. And while we did suffer from soggy clothes and swarms of mosquitoes, we never ran out of food. Nor did we encounter any mysterious strangers.

About the Author

As part of her research for *Frozen Stiff*, Sherry Shahan spent a week camping on the shores of Russell Fjord Wilderness Area and paddled a kayak to Hubbard Glacier. Like the heroine of her story, she battled renegade icebergs and suffered snow blindness.

Sherry Shahan's photojournalistic assignments have taken her riding horseback into Africa's Masailand, hiking a leech-infested rain forest in Australia, and riding in a dogsled for the first part of the Iditarod Trail Sled Dog Race in Alaska.

Sherry Shahan is also the author and photographer of *Dashing Through the Snow: The Story of the Jr. Iditarod*. When not out on an exciting assignment, she kayaks near her home on California's central coast.